THREE BOOKS

Winter in the Country
On "The Death of Ivan Ilyich"
An Atomic Cake

Three Books

Vladimir Azarov

Preface by
Barry Callaghan

EXILE
e d i t i o n s
Publishers of Singular
Fiction, Poetry, Nonfiction, Translation, Drama and Graphic Books

Library and Archives Canada Cataloguing in Publication

Title: Winter in the country ; On"The death of Ivan Ilyich" ; An atomic cake : three books / Vladimir Azarov ; preface by Barry Callaghan.
Other titles: Works. Selections I On "The death of Ivan Ilyich" I Atomic cake
Names: Azarov, Vladimir, 1935- author. I Callaghan, Barry, 1937- writer of preface. I Container of (work): Azarov, Vladimir, 1935- On "The death of Ivan Ilyich." I Container of (work): Azarov, Vladimir, 1935- Atomic cake.
Description: Two books of poetry and a novella.
Identifiers: Canadiana (print) 20190048239 I Canadiana (ebook) 20190048433 I ISBN 9781550968491 (softcover) I ISBN 9781550968507 (EPUB) I ISBN 9781550968514 (Kindle) I ISBN 9781550968521 (PDF)
Classification: LCC PS8601.Z37 A6 2019 I DDC C811/.6—dc23

We gratefully acknowledge the Canada Council for the Arts, the Government of Canada, the Ontario Arts Council, and the Ontario Media Development Corporation for their support toward our publishing activities.

Canadian sales representation: The Canadian Manda Group, 664 Annette Street, Toronto ON M6S 2C8 www.mandagroup.com 416 516 0911

North American and international distribution, and U.S. sales: Independent Publishers Group, 814 North Franklin Street, Chicago IL 60610 www.ipgbook.com toll free: 1 800 888 4741

CONTENTS

PREFACE
by BARRY CALLAGHAN

Vladimir Azarov is in his eighties. He is what I call a *phenom* because he only took up writing seriously a decade ago. Each book is interesting in itself, each is in his voice, yet each is markedly different from the other. It's his voice that is the mystery, it's his voice that is the story, his voice in over a dozen books. Though he is very much a Russian born during the Stalin years and raised in exile in Kazakhstan and bred as a Moscow architect in the grim Brezhnev years, his voice – acquired and honed – is English. He doesn't write first in Russian and then translate into English. He writes poetry in English.

How did this happen?

In a most unlikely way.

Azarov decided back in 2002, though he was part owner of an established architectural firm in Moscow, to leave his country and settle in Canada, in Toronto. His command of English was very limited. He knew German, he knew some French, but English – next to nada! So, what did he do? He decided to learn English by enrolling in a poetry class at George Brown College where he fell into the encouraging embrace of author and publisher Jay MillAr. He began writing poetry, probing his memories of life as he had lived it under a dictatorship, on the fringe of freedom of expression and freedom of movement.

He soon after produced his first full-length manuscripts. Four were published by an English language press in Moscow. And then he published four books in Toronto under the auspices of MillAr. Somehow, these came into the hands of the scholar and first-rate translator from French, Ray Ellenwood. Ellenwood showed them to me and I (having my own fascination with all things Russian: I had studied the language in college), agreed that there was something special there on the Azarov page, something quite distinctive. The next thing we knew, Azarov had two new manuscripts for books on the table, books we at Exile Editions took seriously as English poetry.

The *phenom* was underway. His concerns and his subjects were, of course, fresh and intriguing. In quick succession came five books over three years.[1] Memories of what it had been like "to dare to be happy" as a boy whose parents were in political trouble during the Stalinist regime (his father put to work in a Gulag camp and his mother sent with child-Vladimir to Kazakhstan). What it had been like during the "Thaw," the Khrushchev years when he was an "orphan" student among the "avant-garde" at the Architectural Institute in Moscow (an orphan because he could never acknowledge his prisoner-father). Then what it had been like to design and supervise a cutting-edge institutional building in Mongolia (while somehow travelling for the first time to Berlin, and to Paris, and to London, where, still wet behind the ears, he met Henry Moore); what it was like to see Soviet life through the filter of Catherine the Great; what it was like to celebrate the spirit that resides at the core of great artifice, to celebrate the pioneering artist and aesthetic force of Kazimir Malevich (The Black Square).

And, further to my surprise, he also had translations in mind... Knowing that in the late Sixties and Seventies, when I had come to know Andrei Voznesenski and had translated several Voznesenski poems, Vladimir, full of his eagerness (which is doubly astonishing because ever since I have known him he has been weakened by a cancer), proposed that we work together on translating the very difficult Anna Akhmatova and the almost impossible Alexandre Pushkin. But

---

[1] *Dinner with Catherine the Great, Night Out, Mongolian Études, Seven Lives, Broken Pastries.*

that we did, working line by line for over a year, producing at last an anthology, *Strong Words*, made up of substantial enough selections from those two poets, plus all of my work on Voznesenski.

No sooner had all these books come tumbling out of Azarov, he then responded to the 2014 Sochi Olympics (the town in which he had taken his first holiday as a young man) by falling into a feverish state in mid-winter in his small Toronto flat on King Street. The result? He completed a sixth book for us, *Sochi Delirium*, poems that revolve around, of all people, Marilyn Monroe.

Enough, I thought. This is enough.

Time for a pause in the clock.

How foolish of me. *Of Architecture: The Territories of a Mind* (with illustrations by internationally acclaimed artist Nina Bunjevac) came out in 2016. It is a lively 200-page collection of historical icons, each poem a story about the potency of imagination, territories, border-crossings of the mind – among them: the madness of a king who wants to be a swan, Michelangelo chiselling a heart that beats into his David, Tsar Peter with his three pet dwarfs acting as generals in the army, Vera Zasulich who became the world's first woman terrorist, Robinson Crusoe hunting for the footprints of Friday, Michael Jackson pretending he is Marcel Marceau as he woos Marlene Dietrich in Paris…

And so, what now, what more?

I began to say to myself, "When will the *phenom* strike next?"

Sooner than I thought, and with full force.

Three books in one volume: two of poetry, one of prose.

The novella, *On "The Death of Ivan Ilyich,"* is a fiction rooted in his Moscow life as an architect, where he has entered, as an alter-voice, into that most iconic of Tolstoyan figures, Ivan Ilyich. Death is the subject. Moscow is the place. Wherein Azarov is witness to the withering away of the state of architectural inspiration, the withering away of the imagination itself as a visionary force.

As for the first of the poetry books, *Winter in the Country*, he has boldly engaged those two other voices who bespeak the Russian soul: the beloved Pushkin, father of the language, the archetypal internal exile doomed to die on a point of reckless honour; and Dostoyevsky, the existential visionary, always – with his propensity to gamble – on the nerves' edge of disaster or salvation.

And then, remarkably, in the last book, *An Atomic Cake*, we are given a poetic vision of the stultifying yet often hallucinatory world of post-Stalin Moscow. It was a dank and sometimes freewheeling period under Khrushchev known now as "The Thaw" and under Brezhnev as "The Stagnation," all brought into focus around the image of Rita Hayworth in her negligée as she rode off into the noosphere on the side of an atomic bomb, being tested by the American military on Bikini Atoll in the Marshall Islands.

What all this ads up to, aside from the phenomenal story of an older architect becoming a poet in an adopted language, is a lifetime series of seemingly simple – even guileless – anecdotal memories that provide insights into a world of moral grandeur amidst grotesque expediency, political ruthlessness amidst buffoonery, poetic yearning for transcendence amidst architectural brutalism…all told through memories of a young man who would become who he now is now – a poet with a body of work in English, a *phenom*.

Vladimir Azarov's complete listing of books can be found on page 257.

WINTER IN THE COUNTRY

The second half of a man's life is made up of nothing but the habits he has acquired during the first half.

—F. M. DOSTOYEVSKY

WHAT'S WINTER LIKE IN THE COUNTRY?

1.

What's winter like in the country?
Sasha is seeing snow here for the first time.
A teapot is warming on the stove.
Dark, aromatic, steaming
In a shiny ceramic mug.
Sasha is in good spirits today, looks fresh.
Smiling, rested after a long sleigh ride.
He is here in Mikhailovskoe, province of Pskov,
Exiled, under close watch
Because of his "aetheistic" queries in "a stupid letter."
The house is on his grandfather, Osip Hannibal's estate.
One thousand miles north of the thriving port of Odessa,
City of opera, opulent restaurants (one French), a city of "sound
Reasoning and noble ideas
Concealed," he'd said, "under a soiled
Cloak of cynicism." He'd quit
The city under official duress carrying 389 rubles
Granted him by the court
And another 900 he'd won
In a card game, playing Boston.
Now on the Pushkin family estate,
He is wearing a red shirt
Belted by a sash,
Broad trousers and a fez.

His father, Lev, calls him
Ce monster, ce fils dénature.

Biting cold of a Russian January.
Warmed by his nanny's love –
Cozy and quiet, Sasha on his ladderback
Rush-bottomed chair.
And on the pine table a sheet of paper,
His Cyrillic characters,
His looping line, his quill
Still wet with ink. Sasha angles a suspect word
Off to the margin and, while sipping hot tea,
Starts to read a new stanza to his nanny:

> *...So – we get up, and go to horse.*
> *At a trot, we cut through fields of gorse,*
> *See the sun's first glimmer, agog,*
> *Whip in hand, the yelping of running dogs...*

Nanny, eyes closed, yields to Sasha's rhythms,
His voice, the rhymes. Her eyes hold his
In motherly-like love. She is swaying ever so slightly. To an
Inner music. Blue pours through the frost-mottled pane.
Stillness of the afternoon. A leaden winter day,
Dull lustre of clouds overcast.

Sasha is still sleeping in his
Attic room. He doesn't snore, he sleeps sitting up.
Nanny at the table, a candle burns, tallow burns...

2.

Tired from travel, blizzards.
He's still sound asleep in the afternoon. The whirling of nanny's
Spinning wheel sounds in his sleep
Like insect wings, the same feeling he gets
When he holds his long goose quill...
On this night, Sasha hasn't slept well.
Nanny lit a lamp. Warmed him with a quilt she'd made. Sleep.
A troika had brought him
To her, his loving nanny
In Mikhailovskoe, seat of his childhood summers, autumn leaves.

He loves autumn more than anything.

3.

But now it is winter... Most of the time, he'll stay
With nanny in her coach house hoping to get good work done!
Write, write, write... He might cheer himself up.
Remembering Mikhailovskoe's
Dense green wood, silver sheen off the river.
Wild berries, forest mushrooms...

A small boy. Running barefoot
Through grass wet with dew. Village boys, all
Barefoot. Their raucous but terse country Russian –
Singing words that have become Sasha's words,
Rhymed storytelling, spoken,
A 350-sonnet novel...
Words transformed into his own tongue, his own Russian,
(Now it's our Russian).
Close to his coddling nanny. No, not at his parents' Moscow
Mansion, not anywhere near
His black, French-speaking mother.

4.

A mile-high sky, a big sky, azure blue!
His reedy soprano voice, her muscular
Alto − a duet? −
Baleful songs,
Languid…
Sasha, *Le Nègro du czar,* looked
At her with his soulful eyes.
Then unexpectedly − nanny's heartfelt
Cheerful cry rang out.

Sasha laughed, high-stepping
Around nanny's many coloured skirt.
He squatted, hands on his hips,
Kicking out from under himself, piston legs.
Birches, oaks, plane trees whirling…
Russian fairy tales − so comically different
From the carefully coiffed stories of the
Brothers Grimm. Sasha was excited to learn about
Czar Dadon, and the singing Golden Cockerel;
He wanted to cozy up to the
Beautiful young Ludmila:

> *By the bay by the sea − a green tree grows*
> *A Gold Chain is threaded through its dense foliage*
> *A Cat − who's very smart − is walking around*
> *That Oak and up and down from*
> *Link to Link in the Chain −*

If the Cat goes to the right, he sings Songs
If he goes to the left, he tells Fairy Tales…

January – Sasha is 25.
He's never been this far north, not in the cold season –
And making matters worse, he's in exile.

5.

Sometimes he takes potshots into the woods with his duelling pistol.
All alone, he plays billiards, wagering against himself.

He wrote:
I saw betrayal in every
chance comrade… everyone seemed
to be a betrayer or an enemy… I
grew bitter… tempests raged in
my heart, and hate and dreams
of pale places.

He hasn't been to see his neighbour, an old bachelor
Now retired. As a boy,
Sasha had liked talking to him.
He walks over to
The old captain, through the crisp, shining,
Snow that smells of fir cones.

An old manor off the beaten track.
Still, it is good – snow squalls, carriage wheels,
Carts, hay wagons, matched horses…
His stubborn stride… muddy boots…
Then back home, stretched out on the stove's bench,
Listening to nanny's stories…

6.

Nanny hears the creak
Of old wood, Sasha on the steps
Descending under his crown of curls,
Almost auburn hair. He holds a quill,
Waves a white paper:
"Please, Nanny, listen to my
Poem, it's beautiful:

> *Winter. What's winter like in the country?*
> *My servant's bringing me my morning tea:*
> *What's the weather like? No whistling snowstorms?..."*

7.

"You know, Nanny, he's dead.
Lord Byron. Our beloved Lord of Poetry."

However, Sasha had said in a letter:

The first two Cantos of Don Juan *are*
superior to the rest… everything about
him was back to front: there
was nothing gradual about his
development, he suddenly
ripened and matured — sang and
fell silent and never recaptured
his early notes.

"I like your herbal tea. Listen:

>*Is the sleet gone? Is it time to*
>*Trade in my horsehair settee*
>*For my saddle? I've just visited my boring*
>*Neighbour, thumbing through tedious old journals? But…"*

8.

Nanny brought him a bright lamp and the whistling teapot.
A winter episode. Time stopped:

> *What's a winter morning like in the country?*
> *My servant brings me my first cup of tea:*
> *What's the weather like? Whistling snow? Windy?*
> *Sleet? Is it time to get off the horsehair settee*
> *And get up in the saddle? I've been thumbing*
> *Through my neighbour's old journals, mind-numbing.*
> *Did you tell me there's some fresh fallen snow?*
> *We rise up, and to boots we go and to horse*
> *At a quick trot, cutting through fields of gorse,*
> *See the sun's early glimmer. We're all agog,*
> *Whip in hand, yelping of a running dog…*

"My poor dear. Here's another mug. No milk,
But with a little raspberry from our cold cellar.
You've got a slight cough. Raspberry's a country cure.
Raspberry tea, poor Sasha."

"…I'm reading. Try listening. Don't interrupt!
Please!

> *…Whip in hand, yelping of a running dog*
> *Of a new day!*

"Simple words? Just like the way you talk, my beloved nanny."

...Of a new day! Whip in hand...

And then these lines –

Whip in hand. Yelping of a running dog...
Crossing the grey coulee under the chill
Weight of wet snow, desperate for a kill.
The vespers hour before the storm falls still.
Too late, we missed out on two hares.
A coming blizzard. As a candle flares,
My restive heart longs for something festive.
Bleak with boredom, I sip a digestive.
Book in hand. Take up a quill. Time's short fuse.
Write. Words, words don't work, stalled by my Muse.
Capricious. Ebb and flow I lose
My metaphors, my gift for rhyme. I recuse
Myself to catch up on the communal news:–
Coming elections; a matronly
Hostess scowls at her house menagerie,
Arranging, rearranging cards, it's her art,
She gladly casts my fortune, Knave of Hearts...
Such is country life. Ennui. Distress...
In a quiet corner a game of chess,
A carriage comes to our gatehouse,
It's evening: an old woman, her spouse,
Two girls (two sisters, blond and nicely slim)...

"Nanny please, a drop of Lord Byron's tea, with milk.
One more brief stanza to bring an end to... 'blonde and slim.'

...two girls (two sisters, blond and nicely slim)...
God, such brazen beauty is a sin!
Attentive eyes discreetly meet; then,
A word or two. Then laughter. Talk! And then,
Songs! A small drawing room commotion.
An idle, languid invocation.
At the table, a glance, glint of romance.
At bottom of the outside stair – a torch –
Where a maiden has come onto the porch,
Blouse open at the neck, hair wind-tossed!
Her burning kisses ease the frost!
A Russian maid, a dusting of snow...

I AM WRITING

1.

I thumb through memory's library. Reading, rereading, rewriting
all the writing about writing and more writing about what is all
around me, around my life, the anecdotal whole of my life that I
remember so well, too well, writing without thinking, all of it
interesting for me to read (maybe nobody else?). My vulnerable
soul is on these white pages. Maybe this is the same self-conscious
feeling Fellini had watching his very own subconscious Fellini on the
screen...What can I say?... Fellini is Fellini is Fellini: – getting his
International Movie Prize in the Kremlin – permitted to him when
so little was permitted. An Italian rose on a field of sickles. In the
Sixties... Why a film genius? Why not a writer? Poet? My initial
dream was (how hilarious!) to work within cinema but after my
pre-student visit to the Moscow Cinematographic Institute, in my
young soul, these words appeared:

Good bye to the silent ghostly silver
Coloured dreams of screens!
Good bye Fellini, Eisenstein, Tarkovsky!

And so I live today. Hoping that my editor will publish my
biographical opus. For him, what I'm writing reflects Russian life,
Russian culture. Which he admires? Bearing in mind that my
country's Soviet torture-chamber leaves him in deep melancholy.
I thank him for his unusual love, his enthusiasm.

...I have not written about German, how it is my second language

I have been in Germany, I don't remember how many times – ten, eleven? Probably eight? In the resort town of Ban-Homburg where Dostoyevsky lost all his money. Called ROULETTENBERG in his novel, *The Gambler.* Why don't I write about it? It might be much fresher in my mind than the KGB, their searching, scavenging through our poor place in exile, leading to the arrest of my father, sending him to the Gulag. I was a teenager at that time. Later, after a little more than a decade, I was ready for Germany.

Such amazing cities: Berlin, Frankfurt (Main), Munich, Cologne! Also Dusseldorf! A friend, the architect Guido Dewnissoff, who was still a student at that time... As an innocent abroad, I thought I might helpfully introduce him to the daughter of a Moscow friend, also a student architect. It was a time when many Russian girls dreamed of a foreign marriage...

I, too, was a dreamer. My joy was innocent. I was a tourist.

2.

From May 14 to 24, 1976.

With my limited money, courtesy of the Moscow Tourist Company,
"Intourist" in Germany, I ate only bananas. Or a modest Continental
breakfast in a cheap hotel, where my colleague slept. Bananas! All I ate
all day. Oh bananas! Oh Munich! Dream haven for architects. Even so,
among my most vivid memories of Munich is an American movie I
never would have seen in Moscow: *One Flew Over the Cuckoo's Nest*.
Jack Nicholson speaking fluently in German (thank God, it was
already my second language.). I already knew a little about Nicholson
because of his movie, *Profession: Reporter*. (Antonioni's great cinematic
trick that our Russian, Sokurov, repeated in *The Russian Ark*).

From my first German sojourn, I brought my sick mother a single
kiwi, not available in Soviet food stores. My mother, in bed,
approaching death, was happy to try this subtropical green fuzzy
fruit while asking me about life in Germany after WWII. Was it like
life in the USSR? I was not an expert on degrees of grimness, shades
of dun and grey charcoal.

She had only a rainbow of hopes for me. She was a realist, not a fool
for fantasy, but, nonetheless, she kept hope close to her breast till the
end.

"Don't run to catch the streetcar, the next will come along soon,"
she'd said, seeing me off to Moscow, as I left our exile in Kazakhstan!
Stalin had died, my father was still in the Gulag. Khrushchev wasn't

open to the entire truth. Not at all. Nevertheless, I had the courage to go to Moscow to study. Almost illegally. Following the urging of my brave mother.

"You hear me? Listen! Go. But take care. Think of your weak health. Find a place to heal your back. Your scoliosis. Architect? Architect! Structures! Girders! You were always a sickly boy… Look to your own structure. Poor bones."

We walked to the rail station from the bus stop. She carried my suitcase. I couldn't stop her from helping me. "Who will help you there, my talented curvatured little fool? Visit your Moscow aunts – morose Panya and bubbly Shura. They are afraid because of Shura's husband's military career. Always afraid. They also have a jailed brother. And there's the matter of your father. Lift your left shoulder."

3.

I took my seat on the Moscow train. My mother was on the
platform, her handkerchief to her eyes. She slowly moved counter
to my carriage, away from where Moscow was going to be for me,
wanting to leave me before I left her…

…The Moscow
Special. Quickening
Speed. June rushes by the
Window. Stunted
Steel-green saplings
Windward on the steppes,
Tumbling
Creatures animating my
Cinematic dreams…

Free after ten years of school,
In my pocket, a
Silver medal – emblem
Of my education –

And in my bulky box suitcase that had leather straps,
My father's winter coat
With the karakul collar
(So loved by moths…),
Also a gold medal –
My exam essay about Pushkin.

There was the dangerous matter of my Black Book family story, my father still being behind bars in the Gulag. My mother, though she had dreamed of becoming a judge, had taught me – TO LIE – i.e. about my roots, about who I was; she taught me to write in my student application that my father had disappeared, had never supported his family. Oh my God! Oh my father! Oh my unhappy mother!

4.

Sleepless in the upper berth
Of my rattletrap carriage, memories shaking clear,
The table in our one-room home,
Slices of dark bread under a damp cloth on a plate.
Sitting by our small window. The gloom of a grey early morning
Light pushing through a frost-mottled pane.

> *Earth, blizzard blowing.*
> *Darkness whirling down the sky;*
> *A beast roaring?*
> *Or a baby's wailing cry?*

Vladimir…eat your hard-boiled egg
For breakfast,
Don't forget the salt…

We've left winter behind –
Summer is upon us. I am sitting by the open
Window of a train speeding out of holy Kazakhstan –
Tomorrow morning
I shall be in Moscow, venal Moscow…

A chill wind blows through the carriage. Days of train travel. My
mother is a long way away. I am a long way away from the Asian
edge of the USSR. Days upon days. Mother begins to wait for
news from the great Soviet capital, that severest of capitals…

5.

In my berth, embracing Pushkin's nanny at Mikhailovskoe, reading
through the Pushkin of my secondary school...

A blizzard through the sky.
Whirlpooling dark in the storm's eye;
An airborne beast, it roars, soaring,
Or cries like a baby bawling.

Our rackety old roof of thatched straw;
Shifts and rasps in the storm's maw;
By my window, a ghost walks;
A dead serf, hear how he talks.

Our poor roughcast and fieldstone house
Is sad, stricken by gloom.
Why do you, my loving nanny,
Sit quietly in this tiny room?

Do you fear the racket of the storm?
Are you weary, nanny, dead tired?
Do you dream as you sit all day knitting?
Is your spindle yarn expired?

Where is my fine little drunkard?
Let's toast those years when I was young,
Let us down a bitter tankard
To all the grief that goes unsung.

Sing of how a blue tit dwells
In a dense far-off forest;
Of how a girl walks to a well;
Such delicatesse, so modest.

Swarmed by a swirling storm,
A dark whirling dance.
Roaring beasts, a baby's bawling cry
Resonate a sadness, dread in a trance.

Where is my fine little drunkard?
Youth's gone, but night-time's not so bad,
We drink up to joy, oh nanny,
Our fervent hope – all will be glad!

6.

By 1833, Pushkin has written
"The Queen of Spades."
He is married.
His noble family is impoverished –

Pushkin's Natalie Goncharova is a sloe-eyed Beauty.
Natalie has her admirers.

The Tsar is one of them.
He has said that his name must be written on her dance card,
To waltz with her at the Court Ball
In the Winter Palace where the poet indeed has a
Court position but in fact has little or no money –
Frustration, depression...The Tsar, too, is irritated...
Not good... to have an irritated Tsar...

7.

The feckless joy of a poet's youth!
Faithless friends, flying nymphs!
Childe Harold appears in Cyrillic –
Pushkin is a great poet –
He's a whole village unto himself – a village in political exile,
It's his punishment for glorifying the Peasant, the Russian worker,
His hymns to fresh ruts in the snow
Made by peasant sleigh runners... serfs on the move... all this
From a police report on Pushkin:

At his family's estate, Mikhailovskoe –
His nanny has become his Muse,
Telling him folk tales
And singing songs to him –
The landscape and its serfs
Have become his language...

8.

Admittedly, Pushkin has a mutinous temperament –
He recklessly allowed revolutionaries
To link his name
To the Decembrists
Seeking, I suppose,
A semblance of freedom, even
As he yielded to
The Tsar's censors.

9.

Pushkin's poet of preference – though he is not nearly Pushkin's peer – was
George Gordon Lord Byron, who had become
A bridge of sorts between
Fogbound Albion and…
Waterlogged St. Petersburg.
Pushkin's poetry is a barometer reading of the intellectual continental climate.
French was Pushkin's preferred language,
The language of his aristocratic childhood.
He envied, bitterly so,
Byron's money, his ability to travel through
Turbulent territories,
His life of political flounce.
He feared that he was holed-up
In the backwoods of Russia.

> *Ugh, it is stifling…*
> *Let me regain my sight,*
> *So this is why every night, Refusing to be reconciled*
> *I've dreamed of a dead child.*
> *Yes, yes, that's why…*

Onegin became Pushkin's phantom Childe Harold,
His man on the loose
In Spain, Malta, Albania and Greece!
But Pushkin has never been abroad.
He does not have the Tsar's permission.

In an age of upheavals
And whispers of revolution,
I need permission.

Anyway, he has no money!
Money money! No money. Yet Pushkin refused
A doctored passport proffered
By his friend Pushchin at Mikhailovskoe.
Calling upon the spirit of Lord Byron,
He sat defiantly down and
Drank wine from a dead man's skull.

10.

In January 1825 –
Before the Decembrists showed up in Senate Square,
He quite self-consciously began to play with
A new dream, a new prosaic life
For himself.
A new way of working as an intellectual,
Earning money...
Through a relentless probing on the page of the mind of
Herman, an engineer,
A greedy educated man!
Not a self-indulgent dreamer but a hard-bitten gambler
Ready to kill anyone
Standing between him and money!

In his heart of
Hearts, Pushkin is ashamed!
"I AM NOT HIM!"
But he is! He knows it.
He wears the mask of
Tchaikovsky's melancholy;
In real life
He wants to be his own
Story, his own
Character, the ruthless gambler, Herman...

In 1833, the Queen of Spades sits filing her nails...

WITHOUT A HERO

1.

In a boundless field
My future abounds, still unwritten
But now is stealing – as my remembered past –
Into my Here and Where Will Be, my
Presence in The Future Present.
Which of course is my Past as I now see it
When I was a schoolboy
In Kazakhstan. A good teacher
Told us – intimately, smiling wanly, that
Two hundred years ago
Alexander Pushkin's Lyceum friend –
A future Decembrist – Ivan Pushchin
Came by troika to Mikhailovskoe to visit Pushkin.

2.

Cannon shot of the anti-Tsarist Riots in December!

The squeal and creak
Of crusted snow under
Ivan Pushchin's felt boots as he runs
From his sleigh to the Mikhailovskoe threshold –
And then...
Here I am, the early bird, in my own story
Within this story (or, is it
The other way around?) – at 1 a.m.,
Awake and taking care of myself.
Blinding darkness.
I sleepwalk to my bathroom,
Listen to the erupting flush of my lovely toilet
Installed by that kindest of plumbers,
Greek Peter who's Orthodox,
Who I really like, this honest, hard-working man, and so I give him Russian
Vodka for Orthodox Christmas! –
Seeing myself back to bed,
To dream of opening, if I could, Champagne,
Two glasses, brimming,
Just as Pushkin's nanny is candling the ceiling chandelier,
Crystal glasses on a
Crude pine table –
A sparkling amber in which to seal my dreaming...
A revolutionary fizz –
Veuve Clicquot, or Möet & Chandon, or
Ay-Champagne (St. Petersburg, 1825!)

3.

They drink like peasants from ceramic mugs washed
And dried with a linen towel by
Pushkin's nanny. He calls her Mama

> *With the Widow Clicquot or Möet*
> *Heaven is no idle fable,*
> *Bottles chilled for the poet,*
> *Upright on that crude pine table…*

Three empty bottles (dead soldiers) sunk on
A dark night! And then a pack of
Cards with a Three, Seven, and an Ace…
The Queen of Spades… Discussions, interpretations, presumptions…
The Decembrists… A reputedly wise
Neurologist of the time said the future exists right now, that is,
Deep in the future's ever-present past:
We can feel it in Tchaikovsky, he said,
The urgency of the already experienced moment.

4.

Sasha Pushkin, of course, was an inveterate gambler,
Like most of his rank —
He was a scapegrace aristocrat,
An olive-brown man
With not a ruble to his name:

Money alone brings liberty.
What is Fame. Think nothing of it —
Patch on a poet's rags, so shabby,
We need profit, profit, profit.

He could not avail himself
Of the great gaming halls,
The gold leaf, mother-of-pearl, and baize
Emporiums of the early Nineteenth Century!
He was a rhymester, he was broke,
So he took to writing prose, his heroes, of course, gypsies and
A mad Gambler —

I can clearly see him, he's there, hovering outside
My train-to-Moscow window, caught up
In his mad illusions —
        THREE CARDS
That belonged to an old Countess…

5.

Here's the story – Pushkin needed to gamble.
Poetry is not capital – he needed capital to make
More capital!

*...my grandmother went to Paris, where she was...the "Muscovite Venus,"
...she played faro...she lost an enormous sum...a friend of hers, Count
Saint-Germain – "There is another way of freeing yourself – There is no
need of money. Listen to me..."*

*...She chose three cards in succession, again and again, winning every time,
and was soon out of debt.*

"That's some story," Herman said, "maybe the cards were marked."

"I hardly think so," replied Tomsky...

*So you've got a grandmother who had three winning cards, and you still don't
know what her magic was, her secret...*

Queen of spades –
The old countess – Anna Fedotovna!
A Freudian Death Symbol? No. She is just
An unhappy sick old woman...
Prototype for Raskolnikov, for an old woman's axe-murder...

The past impinges on the present!
Did Dostoyevsky think of Fedotovna?
Footloose as a Mad Gambler
In Roulettenberg
...the chill of it...

Read, my reader, these fractured anecdotes – from and
For – a broken time...

DOSTOYEVSKY LANE

There are things which a man is afraid to tell even to himself,
and every decent man has a number of such things stored away in his mind.

—F.M. DOSTOYEVSKY

1.

The middle of October,
Probably 1940 – I was five –
I stood in line behind my parents
In Moscow waiting to see Great Grandfather Lenin
In his polished granite Mausoleum.
For a couple of weeks my Kazakhstan parents had permission
To travel to Leningrad to sign papers –
Once and for all agreeing to live
As permanent outsiders.

My father had a brother whose family was here in Moscow.
We slept two nights together – six people
In a space of six square metres
Down Dostoyevsky Lane, # 117
In the outlying Marjina Roschta district of Moscow.
I probably remember this because of letters
My parents had written all through WWII
To them, "Our Moscow relatives,"
The letters stopping
Only after my father was sent to the Gulag.

I remember the seemingly endless line...to see Lenin and
I was sure that Grandfather Vladimir Iljich was
Kind, all Soviet kids loved their Grandfathers,
All of us loved him, he lived inside his
Dark polished stone box
And – when I entered his special room,
He – just like in my childhood books –
Smiled at me and gave me a sweet lollipop
Because as a child I had stood in line –
At a time when I was five,
When it was so cold in Moscow – we were
All of us in line, comrades – female and male.
It was probably in October...
Under a drizzly Soviet sky,
Overhanging...

The line is long, straight, slow moving.
No talk, no jokes, no smiling, silence –
Yes, I remember...
Why this crowd? Why am I here?
Why are my parents here?
I am a foolish boy –
My parents will write in their
Kazakhstan report. "No no!
We did not see the Bolshoi nor Tretiakov,
Nor the autumn gold of the Neskuchny Park
But only the mausoleum!
It was so good for our
Honest Soviet souls!"

I am small, smart – two study terms completed together!
I try to relieve my boredom
By exploring the granite skin, the squared stone,
By the architect Alexey Shchusev –
Yes, in my small boy's whirling brain full of
An architectural future.
But HERE AND NOW – this Stone Coffin is dedicated
To our Soviet God – our only GOD …
Such excitement for a five-year-old boy:
"Hooray, Vladimir,"

I cry! Nobody
Repeats my call! My mother
Squeezes my small mittened hand, scared stiff…
Lenin's bodyguards – Red Army soldiers –
Then the sacramental door opened…

Decades have passed…how has it happened,
I am in Moscow again, as an adult…
Probably August. It's 1953 –
I am here illegally: Stalin is dead.
Khrushchev hasn't yet slanged Stalinism…

My poor father is still in the Gulag…

2.

The real Nineteenth-century prophet was
Dostoyevsky, not Karl Marx. —ALBERT CAMUS

I remembered my Moscow relatives –
Down DOSTOYEVSKY LANE, # 117…

Lenin had shared his bedroom – letting them install
A king-size bed for comrade Stalin –
They hadn't been friends
But now Lenin still sleeps with Stalin –
A recurring nightmare in our future…
Two men sleeping together
For all the world to see?

I was a provincial from Kazakhstan,
A Soviet Komsomol member,
A Soviet future student –
This bedroom revelation
Was a little shocking –
All the more so as they were great politicians?
I'd heard rumours of the Bolshoi's
Ballet Boys…their bed dancing…
But our Soviet Revolutionary leaders?

I entered into holy Moscow for the second time…

In a deep sleep I am five again...
117, down Dostoyevsky Lane
My mother tries to wake me...
She pulls long warm socks up over shins...
"Get up, get up" – she whispers, afraid
Of wakening my cousin, Lyusya
Who is also small like me, but six...
As a Muscovite, she did not have to hurry off to Kazakhstan...
"Dear," my mother whispers, "we need
To catch the early streetcar
To Kazan Station... Oh please...
Open your eyes, Vladimir, my dear son..."
So you can see the darkness
Behind the crocheted lace of the
Cross-ribbed window pane...

My Uncle Peter's wife told my mother;
"Lyuba, this morning is so cold.
There's ice on the puddles –
Take Lyusya's fur coat for Vladimir until you get to the Station...
See – it's so warm –
My old rabbit coat..."

"Thank you, dear Proskovia" – my mother whispers...

Lyusya yelped.

"My loving fur-r-r!
My Moscow fur does not want to go to Kazakhstan!
I hate you, you awful boy, Vladimir! You are a Kazakh!"
Lyusya, Lyusya! Muscovite…

In 1953 I ran to my relatives, lonely in Moscow…
117 Dostoyevsky Lane –
My mother:
"Visit our relatives right away. You'll be
Hungry – they'll give you food…"

My mother also told me:
"Your Uncle Peter's wife, Proskovia, she
Is very tough… You know –
When he was young and handsome – our Uncle Peter,
He kidnapped her from a Gypsy encampment…
Because she was gorgeous, a Gypsy-Queen –
My son, be respectful, call her Proskovia Ioannovna…"

Moscow relatives, six metres of rooms
Two male cousins –
Vineamin and Yuri – A sister Lyusya –
Inside six metres…

I am near now, the streetcar
Passing old ugly houses,
NUMBER – 117:
A brick first floor
An upper floor made of wood
Standard Maryina Roscha architecture…

Opening into the semi-darkness of a staircase.
A slip of a silhouette
A slim girl... Lyusya.

"Hello! You are Vladimir!
Welcome to Moscow!
Exams are over?
In the summer I
Work for a food store, selling sausage."

(SAUSAGES? A holy word! We never had
Sausages in Kazakhstan...)

"This September
I'm taking my second course – at
The Engineering Institute here,
Near home – it's so convenient...
I intend to build Bridges and Tunnels –
You are a pure architect... Yes?
Your buildings will surround me! On the
Banks of all the Russian rivers..." –

An August wind lifts
Lyusya's light blond curls off her neck –
I'm happy to have this young cousin
With her soft sing-song Muscovite lilt,
A dialect that is so beautiful. I will
Never be able to talk like that... Not
After my Kazakh upbringing...

I think of my new friends in Toronto
Whose English is so good...
Ewan and Siobhan... And Lyusya!
Her pastel-coloured silk dress
That her father had brought by military mail train
From Germany –
The Moscow Princess and the Kazakh Prince...

3.

Striding through
Red Square hiding who I am –

Walking through Maryina Roscha,
Passing down Dostoyevsky Lane – settling
Into that dormitory – the suburban mansion
Of that merchant philanthropist,
Patron of the arts – Savva Mamontov...
Then, I lived near the VDNKH, the
Soviet Agricultural Exhibition –
In the shadow of that internationally known sculpture,
Working Man and Peasant Woman by Mukhina –
Bourdelle's student in Paris before
The Great Russian Revolution ...

Dostoyevsky Lane is what drew me:
Uncle Peter was a pleasant man...
I went with him to the Soviet Army Park
In the same district – and sometimes
We went to the pond to where the scullers were,
And sometimes we ourselves would row, talking family,
Avoiding any mention of my father, of course,
But we spoke about my grandparents –
Their village, Tula –
Great-grandfather Timothy
(Andreevich) – father of uncle Peter and my father...
Our only Azarov (here my uncle laughs) CAPITALIST –

Owning early in the Twentieth century
A construction company,
He had two houses on Lusinovskaya Street in the
District of Moscow, being a new merchant character right out
Of one of Dostoyevsky's novels, or Ostrovsky's plays…

"Vladimir! 1917 came too soon…
Our young capitalist grandfather couldn't send any
Of us off to the Sorbonne or to Cambridge,
Like many nouveau riches did at the time…
You, Vladimir, are our only hope,
Our future architect…"

Oh no, dear uncle! I'll never make
Money, I'll never have a heavy purse…
In my early years, ever since I was ten, my passion was drawing,
And painting –
I invented artificial oil, several colours,
Out of Kazakh agricultural chemicals…
Don't smile…those were my teens, dear uncle!
You might remember?
You sent me small
Paint tubes in a box from Moscow – right after WWII –
And I did a couple of genuine oil études!
My mom sent back,
Because you were all so hungry here in Moscow,
A parcel of buckwheat
With firmly-packed jam, blackcurrant…

Vladimir… Life is life… Everything's okay, we
Are alive… Our great neighbour, Fyodor Mikhailovich, said:

Man is unhappy because he doesn't know he is happy,
That's the only reason. That's it!…"

4.

I found great happiness in
My uncle's ruined district, Maryina
Roscha… With its monstrous tilted houses,
Two-storeys of
Brick and rotten logs, out of some scene in
Dostoyevsky, but then,
All his melancholy novels
Are set in St. Petersburg…fog, grey weather, ice,
Depression clinging to the town,
Our rainy northern capital…
I am, without warning, returned to confront # 117 –
An ugly house, where my
Uncle Peter's family resides…
Dangerous stairs to the second floor…
To enter a common hallway
With a gas stove in the belly of the room –
A common kitchen for all neighbours,
Probably ten people…
All friends!
Fantastic! The same choric "Hello!"
An old grey man. Single, as I remember…
About sixty, maybe younger – very quiet
Cooking kasha, cooking millet grain –
Then, an aging couple – a plump wife
And her beaming big-toothed husband who helps her cook supper…
They'd lost a son during WWII…
A neighbour, Irina, smiling but

She looks at me with a hint of guilt...
I've never heard a bad word about her
But she is a prostitute –
(Peter and Proskovia's kids
Don't know the word yet –)
She is *"Bed-and-Breakfast."*
Bringing in clients from
The Moscow East Kazan Railway Station –
Soviet Muslim men coming to Moscow:
Turkmens, Uzbeks,
Tadzhiks, and my own "friends" – Kazakhs –
This evening she has a day off
And is hovered over on her dessert on the gas stove –
I hear voices behind Uncle Peter's door...

"The novels of Dostoyevsky are seething whirlpools, gyrating sandstorms,
waterspouts which hiss and boil and suck us in. They are composed purely
and wholly of the stuff of the soul. Against our wills we are drawn in,
whirled round, blinded, suffocated, and at the same time filled with a giddy
rapture. Out of Shakespeare there is no more exciting reading."

—Virginia Woolf

Near door, more dialogue
From down Dostoyevsky Lane:

The Devil is fighting with God – the field of battle is the hearts of the people.

Yes, that's Dostoyevsky...

PETER:
Leave him alone, our unhappy little boy who has no father!

PROSKOVIA:
Don't forget your own children! Lyusya, thank God,
Doesn't need anybody's attention!

PETER:
Since WWII, my wife's been
In Moscow – a German Fraulein, God bless my mail train to
Berlin…

PROSKOVIA:
Why are you lavishing respectful attention on this exiled student
in front of your own two sons? Yes, he is your nephew. There's a
reason why we're in such danger all these years! I can't sleep! Your
brother's in the Gulag! You are a Soviet Military officer! And this
gift you gave him – this German silk blue shirt. It's too expensive.
Your sons don't have anything like that. This is awful!

PETER:
Human beings are more expensive than money.

PROSKOVIA:
You've never gone rowing with Venianim and Yuri. Why are you
out strolling around town with Vladimir, going through Red Army
Park? Our neighbours told me…

PETER:

About the Gulag, about my brother, when he was here in 1940, he said: "*All of them, because they cannot lead their business properly, like to blame us a lot, especially for spying.*"

PROSKOVIA:

You fool! Don't say anything. The door's open!

I left that Moscow kitchen hallway. My legs shaking...

This note of personal feeling, this harsh reality of actual experience, undoubtedly gives "Humiliated and Insulted" something of its strange fervour and terrible passion, yet it has not made it egotistic; we see things from every point of view, and we feel not that action has been trammelled by fact, but that fact itself has become ideal and imaginative. —Oscar Wilde

5.

Dirty Bozhedomka Street,
A truly Dostoevskian part of town...
In the Hospital where his doctor father had worked,
Where he a great writer, had been born!
Down his Lane toward
Bozhedomka Bridge –
Which sounds so silly in Russian, almost indecent:
"The house for the people of God...
The insane, ill, poor, vagabonds, tricksters, etc. –
A cemetery here for those who couldn't make a living in this
Blessed world and committed suicide.

In 1805 the mother of Alexander the First founded the first
Hospital for the very poor here. Dostoyevsky's father was a doctor
from St. Petersburg, where his son, Feodor, was born, where, in
1928, Soviet Power established his Museum.
Where I am now, reading from a marble slab, hardly visible, in the
shadow light:

The F.M. Dostoyevsky Museum Apartment is located in the former
wing of Mariinsky Hospital for the Poor. The family of doctor M.A.
Dostoyevsky, father of the future writer, occupied a small apartment
consisting of two rooms on the ground floor. F.M. Dostoyevsky, who was
born in the opposite wing, lived in this apartment from 1823 to 1837.

When I was young I was very very
Hungry, wanting Proskovia's soup,
Waiting for Lysya to come home from the Institute.
I was tired but so hungry…
The sun went down.
A grim frost
Numbing my hands.
Dusk fell.
Across the street
I caught sight of an old man and
His dog. The bakery shone,
An ice-bound neon lustre.
I stopped fingering my money,
Feeling some awful presentiment
About how it was with us who
Were living in our time,
Seeing
The stooped old man,
His slow,
Faltering gait, pushing forward on stilt-like legs,
So thin, tapping the paving stones
With his stick…

…I had been feeling unwell since morning, and by evening I was distinctly
worse, with a fever coming on. Besides, I had been on my feet all day and I
was tired. Evening came… I love the sun, especially the setting March sun…
on a clear frosty evening. The whole street is suddenly bathed in brilliant
light. All the houses glow. For a time, the grey, yellow and dull-green façades
lose their drabness; there's a sense of euphoria, of awakening, as though

someone had poked you in the ribs. The sun's rays vanished. The frost was getting sharper and beginning to numb my nose. Dusk was falling…

The front door down Dostoyevsky Lane slammed shut behind me. I was outside, having taken the rickety house stairs two at a time… The cold March evening subdued me. An indigo light in the Lane… Weak lamps had burned out. Walking fast…going nowhere, no thoughts… Down Dostoyevsky Lane…

I hated how everything was. My being a student at a prestigious, almost aristocratic, art school, yet living in humiliating, insulting circumstances. The Stalinist regime hung over my life. Every day I waited for shocking news. Hearing the euphemisms for "disappearance" in my head. In the Institute. In my dormitory.

And here, too, so close to my simple, even dull-witted yet terribly kind relatives. Am I exaggerating? Millions of people living their life in the mighty USSR of Fear? Am I a fool? Are my relatives weak people – swamped by anxiety, grief, uncertainty…deeds secretly done years ago…?

What time is it now? Ten-thirty? There, in the right corner of my laptop – 2015-03-03… I'd forgotten about breakfast! My morning exercises! My chiropractor… Look, it is snowing in the yard behind my Toronto home! Not in Moscow, not in Kazakhstan… but here in Toronto! Where I am trying to snatch signs of what was from forgetfulness. I need a break from the monotone of my clapping keyboard…so I move my chair, go to the kitchen…yes, yes, yes…it's okay…

Am I unhappy because I don't know I'm happy?

Dostoyevsky's *The Gambler* is on my desk:

Remember my precept: invent neither a plot, nor an intrigue, take what life gives to you by itself. Life is much richer than all our fabrications! No act of imagination can give you what you get from everyday ordinary life... Respect life!

Yes! Dostoyevsky, your precept is my method... Life is a dictator dictating my fractured life to me. Plain and simple – even primitive... Gertrude Stein! Tell me once again: "*One must dare to be happy.*"

EPISTLE TO GREATER GERMANY

And other thought is misfortune
  Is death and night to me:
I hum no supportable tune,
  I can no poet be.
          —JOHANN WOLFGANG VON GOETHE

1.

My mother held a kiwi in her weak hand. She smiled. This was in
Moscow; my father had died in his eighties, my mother was in the
palliative care of my sister, Nina. We would bury her, birches bent
over Lyubov Mikhailovna Azarova...

A modest cement marker. Every year I go there. With flowers. My
sister weeds the mound.

That kiwi was eaten in the Seventies. I was to somehow go about
entering greater Germany as a Soviet architect. A huge Soviet
Project! Our team had secured a new contract!

It was a dream. We wanted to live a little, wanted to be better off
behind our curtain of iron – an illegal dream. We wanted to earn
foreign money. Another, illegal dream. Yet, I knew and treasured
Gertrude Stein: "*One must dare to be happy.*"

And now:

HOW ABOUT A SHALOM ALEICHEM STORY?

Two Kiev guys came to
    Germany wanting to grow the threadbare
        Post-war
        Jewish population.
    One of them, Villy
        (In Kiev, he was like me – Vladimir),
    Settled down in madcap Berlin.
His wife was a hairdresser.
        A pomade and bouffant innovator
Who had hoped to backcomb fraus at their roots,
        Turn them into elegant Soviet Ukrainians, our
            LADIES of the Steppes

For the moment, all her customers were
        From the Ukrainian community,
Along with a couple of crones from Moscow.
The second guy – well-known at the time – was a Soviet
    Kiev football player, Yakov.
        Single, young enough,
    He meditated upon the state of his abs,
    His hamstrings,
Kept his body flexed, honed.
    He ended up on the prowl
    For a patron
        In the German South,

In Bad Toltz spa country!
Indoor waves of curative mineral waters,
  Whirlpools!
    Aquariums for fat people!
    Heated toboggans!
    And –
    Gambling casinos!
   Casino this! Casino that! Gold leaf!
Yakov settled in the town
 Dostoyevsky called ROULETTENBERG…where, D.
After a visit, with not a rouble in his pocket and deeply in debt,
Was forced to write, hunched over his desk, a novel;
  THE GAMBLER!

2.

Dostoyevsky is…the only psychologist from whom I've anything to learn.

—Friedrich Nietzche

Muller Horex Company had joint-partnered with
The Soviet Organization Project, where I was, though not a
Communist, deeply involved.
Meeting up with German and Austrian advisors and entrepreneurial specialists,
I was happy! Go-lucky. In West Berlin's Ka De We department store
I bought, as an escapee from Soviet tawdriness, a coat of London Burberry!
Which I still wear in Toronto
    (slightly shortened!... to fit my shortening life
In my new country).

At the edge of the Odenwald mountains
Where, let us say, an "aggressive" black wine is made on the
North slope
And a gentle, slightly sweet wine is made on the
Sunny south slope,
I attended a tasting
At a villa owned
By our corporate Boss, the architect,
Herr Hoeniger!
He was elegantly groomed, a handsome man. I am still
Jealous of his beige tweed jacket,
Its leather buttons…

Beethoven's quartets
In his car on his car radio,
An accompaniment to condescending questions:
"Take a guess, Vladimir, my little Moscow architect.
What's the number of this quartet? Not Sixteen, no!
Sixteen was his Last.
You're almost right – Fourteen. Thank you…"
      (An aside –
Back home on a shelf in our Kazakh flat, my father
Had kept *Hütter's Metallurgy Technology* –
Five books in German, and a Bible,
Books that travelled with him to the camps.
To the last circle of Stalin's Inferno.
Later, my mother gave those books to some Soviet Kazakh college –

3.

...a road leads up
To the fairy-tale villa
Of our enabler and host – Herr Hoerniger –
We approach under the eye of his security cameras –
His solar-powered villa,
An electronic roof – lives detected,
Regulated, computerized, controlled –
High-tech intimacy of the early Nineties –
"This is a UNESCO building –"
Herr Hoerniger told us during our wine tasting
Wines from opposite slopes of the mountain – black and white, vintage.

Herr Hoerniger calling out toasts:
"To our Russian guests! To you! To you! To you!
Also – to you, Vladimir! Our youngest!
You have a family already? And kids?
So nice! A son! Perfect! How old?
What? Thirty?!
YOU!!! ARE – Vladimir – THIRTY!!!
(Much raucous laughter)
Your German is not perfect. Translate for him, Yakov, translate
My question..."

Yakov, a Kiev sportsman, amiable, who smiles a lot –
As the ingratiating aide to Herr Hoerniger.
After a couple of glasses of vino, he whispers in my ear:
"I promise I'll show you the casino, some real gambling,

Some real gamblers and in the real Roulettenberg
Where Feodor Dostoyevsky's portrait is still where it should be,
On the wall…"

4.

"...My brows were damp with sweat, and my hands were shaking. Also,
Poles came around me to proffer their services, but I heeded none of them.
Nor did my luck fail me now. Suddenly, there arose around me a loud din of
talking and laughter.

"Bravo, bravo!" was the general shout, and some people even clapped
their hands. I had raked in thirty thousand florins, and again the bank had
had to close for the night!

"Go away now, go away now," a voice whispered to me on my right. The
person who had spoken to me was a certain Jew of Frankfurt – a man who
had been standing beside me the whole while, and occasionally helping me in
my play..." —DOSTOYEVSKY. *The Gambler*

Not Baden-Baden's palaces
Where Dostoyevsky had often gambled.

No. A modest provincial gambling house
In Bad Hamburg.

Semi-darkness. A framed portrait well-lit,
Signed:
Feodor Michailovich Dostoyevsky –

"Yes, for God's sake go," whispered a second voice in my left ear. Glancing
around, I perceived that the second voice had come from a modestly, plainly
dressed lady of rather less than thirty – a woman whose face, though pale and
sickly-looking, bore also very evident traces of former beauty. At the moment, I
was stuffing the crumpled banknotes into my pockets and collecting all the

gold that was left on the table. Seizing up my last note for five hundred
gulden, I contrived to insinuate it, unperceived, into the hand of the pale
lady. an overpowering impulse had made me do so, and I remember how
her thin little fingers pressed mine in token of her lively gratitude. The
whole affair was the work of a moment.

Then, collecting my belongings, I crossed to where trente et quarante
was being played..." —DOSTOYEVSKY. *The Gambler*

Shivering. I am in a
Gambling house for the first time. A word,
CASINO, in rainbow colours.
The interior exudes decades of dinge,
The colours of corruption. Grey-lilac curtains of
Thread-bare velvet. Downscale bordello,
Zola's "Nana..."
...slim female figures –
Long silver gowns, vapid faces,
A pale powdered joyless sparkle...

5.

"Come, come, Vladimir!"
Whispers Yakov –
"Look, a real painted Dostoyevsky portrait and
Real live girls from a real Tahitian Island.
I'll tell you the whole story later…"
Yakov gave each of us money – Deutch
Marks – in addition to our salary for the trip –
I spent those marks on
A cheap radio, a mini Grundig for my schoolboy
Son – so did we all – Soviet business travellers!!!!
The Tahitian girls stopped by to say hello
In the main gambling salon.
Dolls,
Inviting, soft, but still they are very
Serious, an almost metallic aura about them.
I had dreamed
In Moscow of reading
How to Win Friends And Influence People
(How unknowing I was),
That Dale Carnegie book –
This girl, I thought, might become
A friend from Tahiti! She is
Taking off her Polynesian
Post-Impressionistic colours, a touch of Gauguin,
So slim, trembling, but vibrant,
As if clean, cold Bavarian air could come

From a hot country, tilting her little chin
Under Der Ring des Nibelungen – here she was, fruition of
Gauguin's sin…?

In my faulty German:
"Are you not the great…great-granddaughter
Of a…a…
Great French artist who had a young Tahitian
Girl as his wife and model –
Tehara was her name?
Perhaps she was your grandmother?"
Straw hut, bright banana leaves that have
Become oranges at the D'Orsay
Station, brave Tahitian girl. I immediately invited her to the Soviet Union
As a prospective worker, yes, yes,

In our proletarian country! Innocent that I was, quivering…
Fingering Yakov's Deutch Marks in my pocket…

BALLAD OF SASHA (A PLAY IN DREAM)

Oh write it not, my hand —
The name appears already written.
Wash it out, my tears!
                    —ALEXANDER POPE

Characters:

Chorus (St. Petersburg high Society)
Sasha (the Great Russian Poet)
Natasha (his Wife)
Catherine (her Sister)
Georges-Charles (Sasha's Brother-in-Law)
Tsar (of all the Russians)
Death (of Sasha) —

The Scene is a Black Brook near St. Petersburg,
    on January 27, 1837

1.

CHORUS:
Here let us stand as witness to the event. Here, let us wait,
Drawn to danger.
We live to invent the reasons for what happens –
Call it Rumour, Gossip, Hearsay, Tittle-Tattle,
Whispers, Canards (loose lips? – a strange invention…)
No – to us, it is like a public sharing from the heart,
Innocence having its own wisdom.

We live in a cold country –
Burning burning burning –
So, we begin on a cold northern January day…
Events mount up as imperceptibly as falling snow…
Becoming the abscess of an ill life –
Natasha, her sister Catherine,
Their new-found French brother-in-law, together
Begin to painfully open a wound.

SASHA:
A few days ago I saw my own death
Crawling toward me
As I played this dangerous game twenty-six TIMES –
Gambling is a kind of suicide…
Living my aristocratic life with
No money! I got involved in duels;

SIX! I am a good shot!
I smiled at her, this eyeless, noseless slut (that's how Akhmatova will call her):

When will you come to me, Death?
In my time of onerous fighting?
Or while sailing the waves?
Or when a volley of shot will
Cause my cold ashes?

2.

DEATH:
As usual, I search for him – our
Sasha in a fur coat sitting
On a snowdrift
Waiting for the END –
I remember
His words:

> *Every hour steals and steals and steals our life.*
> *But we are still together,*
> *Believing we are alive....*
> *Death comes softly without warning...*

Come, come, come –
To your loving nanny! Arina Podionovna!
At Mikhailovskoe,
In this cold, heartless season...
Black Brook...frozen, powdered snow...
Bare trees, silhouetted men:
Your French brother, the killer, the hired
Seconds
They are READY to engage in a cosmic act –
The Eternal Recurrence, darkness
Of the Black Brook!

CHORUS:
The rock of God beneath their feet!
Trampled on by four men, the snow is
Endless, bright scarlet
Blood,
Purple stomach wound...
The cowardly sun hides behind the clouds,
Ashamed –
SASHA IS NO MORE...
The Seconds – the minutes, hours – fled.
He'd been brought by sleigh –
And then two days of
Blood seeping into his bed sheets –

3.

TSAR:
(from a letter to the Tsar's sister, Anna Pavlovna, wife of Prince William of Orange)

I must inform you of a tragic event
Which ended the life of
Our notorious poet – please, do not talk this about…

CHORUS:
Sasha's body
Buried secretly, far from St. Petersburg. His papers sealed – No obituaries…

DEATH:
He is dead – I confirm this!
He pounds his fist
On my door…
Welcome home, Sasha!

CHORUS:
We were curious when Sasha left his St. Petersburg house this afternoon
To fight a duel with his new brother-in-law, Georges-Charles, a Frenchman,
An Officer of the Tsar's Horse Guard, known to be a crack shot…

DEATH:
…my boring daily duty, the feeding
Of old men and women into the mouth
Of the Earth.

GEORGES-CHARLES:
I was welcome here once, in this cold country –
The Tsar loves me as my paternal Baron de Heeckeren loves me.
I became a Baron, too!
I am a fashionable Military dandy!
Looming over ordinary men and women!
But this poet – this gossipmonger, this rabble-rouser,
This intellectual insurgent!
I need to kill him!
[Pause]
Back! Back! Back. Away
From this rude barbaric Russian winter!
I hope to
Escape this world's wild vengeance...
To PARIS!
This Poet. I hate
This impatient black bully –
A fool! A poor unhappy cuckold!
A great Russian rhymester?
No matter.
His wife loves the beauty of my presence!

DEATH:
I hate this vicious affected French fool!
I loathe seeing him in my world.
I wait to take him when he comes crawling all alone.
On his knees! Asking –
Pleading –

4.

NATASHA (Sasha's Wife):
Sasha! Where are you? My poor boy with your short fuse.
Washing, shaving, putting on
Eau de Cologne?
Sasha, you cannot keep your African temper under control.
All society
Blames me, your wife...

DEATH:
A bug-eyed lecherous Frenchman!
Get your dirty deal done.
Idiot! Kill Sasha for me...

SASHA:
Why did I encourage Georges-Charles to play such a foul role?
I knew who he was...
Why did I kill the poet Vladimir Lensky?
Answer me, Evgeny! Onegin! YOU are ME!
Why kill a poor young poet!
Our family is quite mad:
I can't blame
Natasha's sister, Catherine. She dreamed of being
His wife!

CATHERINE:
I loved him, madly! Forgive me, Sasha, Natasha!
I loved him more than my own life!
This handsome young soldier...

SASHA:
Catherine's fatal mistake.
We cannot live without error.
Why did I kill Vladimir Lensky?

5.

SASHA:
Answer me, Onegin. You shot him!
YOU ARE ME!
Why, Evgeny, did you kill Vladimir?
It's all so confusing!
Maybe I am Vladimir, not you –
I sit very still:

Not moving, his forehead damp, cold,
Languishing, chest wounded,
Only an instant before
His heart was pulsing –
Life was at play, blood boiled!
Now, his heart, his home, is dark and quiet;
Shutters closed, windows
Painted white. No mistress.
Not a trace of her, gone…

CHORUS:
Let us stand close by. Let us wait.
Drawn to St. Petersburg society.
They are no danger to us.
We live to witness,
To invent reasons for such events.

6.

CHORUS:
Sasha was killed close to the Black Brook.
A loud shot, snowflakes fell, birds fly
Far from the Tsar's Palace. He had not tried to stop the murder.
He'd worried about Sasha's trouble-making.
He could have exiled the great poet's
Brother-in-law, Georges-Charles,
Back to Paris. He could have
Ordered Natasha's
Sister – Catherine – to follow her husband.
Miserable, she died trying to give
George-Charles a fourth child.
He'd met the beautiful Natasha
On a Paris bridge...out for a stroll with his son
Who was still a boy... George-Charles said quietly –
        "Natasha"...
His son wrote
About this ghostly bridge
In his memoirs...also about his poor sister
Who couldn't bear to live knowing that
Her father had murdered the ultimate Russian genius...
She had studied Russian
So that she could read Sasha's poetry!
In her madness – poor child! –
She committed suicide...

Birds sing… Trees are green in the spring…
Babies cry coming into the light…
Water is winter ice…

In the Name of the Father, the Son,
And the Holy Ghost… Amen…

WHERE PUSHKIN'S NEVER BEEN

Blizzard storming...

1.

Snowstorm blizzard,
Whirlpooling darkness;
A beast, it roars;
Cries like a baby...

A dark blue Kazakh evening behind the
Small crossed window panes –
In the whirlpooling snow nothing is visible
Of the polluted Soviet
COAL MINES of the Kazakh –
Lunar hills – gas tails, flames on the slopes.
Kazakh black energy,
Carbon.
Diamond formed from carbon by the Kazakh
Town of Karaganda
Of the Soviet Republic! Stalin's era!
My teenager lungs, I am coughing.
The ecology of our social being.

2.

A clean quiet settlement.
My father,
After being arrested
Was taken out of this town to a jail
Where an investigation of
NOTHING was conducted...this was before his launch
Into the nowhere of the Gulag...
An Emperor With No Clothestime
Though no one could yet see the pale bare body...
The Brothers Grimm, with their historical, political satire, their
Joke – their dark laughter!
For us, Generalissimo Stalin – was no joke.

My father's family,
With their goods, chattels, ending up in
This coal mining wasteland...
My mother standing in an endless line to get to the
Bars of the jailhouse window...
Sorrowful martyrs all across Russia...
Starting in the Thirties my mother, while still very young,
Stood in line on a wet windy Leningrad winter day –
My father, a diploma student,
Arrested for the first time...
His soul still alive with his dream of
Designing a new Soviet flying machine
Capable of great distance
Around the world and

Into outer
Space.
He, a true believer in the
Communist religion,
Trapped...
So many thousands of secret-sharers in the Thirties...

3.

My mother stood in line
Like Anna Akhmatova in Leningrad:

> *One day someone "identified" me.*
> *Then a woman blue with cold standing behind me,*
> *Who of course had never heard my name, roused herself*
> *From the stupor common to*
> *Us all, and whispers in my ear:*
> *"Can you describe this?" –*

> *I never sought asylum among aliens*
> *Never cowled myself in a crow's wings.*
> *I stood as people stood, alone –*
> *In my marrowbones, their sorrow.*

My mother had worked hard, studied zealously,
Preparing for the red horizon of the future!
Time crawls yet flies. Now, it's the Kazakh Fifties –
My mother's life,
Decade by decade, gone…
We are in Karaganda!
She's found a job in a food store:
Cleaning BUTTER – yes, what had been butter!
(Tons of real butter that had gotten old
And had gone OFF).
Her work? – to scrape
The green mould that clung to the big blocks

From what had been
Fresh butter.
She had also found
Accommodation.
A small brick house in a built-up area of
Our coal town
Where I sat by a small window, watching
A Kazakh blizzard,
Memorizing Pushkin for my morning class:

Whirlpooling darkness in the sky;
A beast, it roars;
Or cries like a baby...

4.

Early evening. My window is
Almost a midnight blue.
Mother had turned the owner of this house into her friend.
They worked at the same job – the restoration of Aged Soviet Butter.
A cat is nearby. Black and white spots.
Peaceful. So quiet in
Our room – which is
A kind of entrance hall.
I hear the ticking clock from
The next big room where the landlady lives with
Her two daughters…
The cat lies on my cold lap
To warm me up.
I repeat Pushkin's lines:

> *Whirlpooling darkness in the sky;*
> *A beast, it roars…*
> *Or cries like a baby…*

5.

My mother and the landlady
Are friends, of a kind.
I remember coming home from school. Late,
I was surprised to see my mother playing
Cards with the her.
My mother smiled, sheepish, seeing my confusion.
I didn't know that she'd ever gambled.
But there she was.

And then I heard:
"Please, Lyuba, go
To bed early tonight. My girls
Went to their grandmother's.
Vasili, he's coming tonight…"
I was lying on my aluminum cot.
My light, a single hanging bulb.
A different light poured in from the
Room of the landlady's business partner in the house –
She was waiting for her man –
I was waiting, curious, fearful,
A drunkard was coming…
Pushkin in my head:

*A beast, it roars
Or cries like a baby…*

6.

A loud knock! Knock! A very loud knock!
A boot put to the door.
Our landlady ran
In her perfumed long silk robe…
A lunatic noise:
Our landlady screamed:
"Ah-a-a-ah! The pain! Stop! Please!"
"Shut up and move your ass – faster,
Foolish fucking whore! Move! Fuck! Fuck! Fuck!"

She was left crying, crawling, beaten
By the fists of her lover…
Their door shut!

Poor Pushkin had to listen in my head
To those obscene oaths, that scream!
Orgiastic oaths beating
Under my blanket on
Aristocratic eardrums,
As he himself had cried out in his wild Ethiopian voice to
His rival, Baron George-Charles de Heeckeren d'Anthès,
Frightening his wife, the beautiful Natasha,
Who had kept quiet
As my mother kept very quiet, very still,
As if absent in her own room in the house
Listening to me repeat my class poem, my beloved
Pushkin's words:

A blizzard storming the sky,
Whirlpooling darkness...

Darkness in the sky...
Whirling like a dark beast...
         ...it roars;

Or cries like a baby...

Reminding the...
...beast...the dark beast of the dark light
of a sweetness at the heart...

...shining metal horns appeared –
A military cap with a red star between the horns.
The pawing of his right hoof:
Pushkin smiled at me...stood near...

GOD IS DEAD:
A HALLUCINATION

All theory is grey, my friend.
But forever green is the tree of life.
    —JOHANN WOLFGANG VON GOETHE

1.

This girl is in Rome, or Paris, or Berlin –
Ignore her, let her go – she was or will be
One of those who are
Transient in all of Europe,
A beautiful young lady, coming
To Rome from St. Petersburg
With her doting mother
To present herself, reveal herself – proudly.

So the young lady is drinking strong black coffee
At Café Greco owned by the
Greek, Nicola Della Maddalena.
Her mother, having read about this place in
Corriere della Sera, is urging her daughter
To drink coffee with
Sarah Bernhardt, Puccini, Verdi,
At a round marble table while holding
An open book, not forgetting to
Smile, to be, at all costs, attractive...

Her mother, sitting separately. Later, asking:
"Why did you talk so long to the young man with
His oh so sweet, oh so gentle manners?"

"Mother, he is very special! He studies
Psychology – such a new
Perspective, such a new science!"

"Do you want to heal mad persons? With their dangerous
Incurable diseases? You should be a Princess,
With your beauty, stunning among successful men?"

"This branch of knowledge is paramount now, dear mother!
Everyone who is a leader, who fights for power
Will owe obeisance to this new science, this cosmos!
To be so close to someone of genius is bizarre,
Psycho-patient – poor man – who loves horses,
NIETZSCHE...
Oh mother, you can read all about him in *Corriere della Sera*..."

2.

GOD IS DEAD – he said – Gott ist tot!
Dead are all gods…
We have become
Free creatures with the power to become ourselves!

1883-1885
Friedrich Nietzsche's *Thus Spoke Zarathustra*

You must be ready to burn yourself in your own flame…
How could you become new, if you had not first become ashes?

Nobody holds his own ashes
We do not think about our ashes…
Zarathustra speaks –

WHAT IS GREAT IN MAN IS THAT HE IS A BRIDGE
AND NOT AN END…
Ashes constitute
Our very distant Future!
God is dead! We lived Yesterday in our Tomorrows!
We are Living Now!
Our ashes are a bridge
Over a dead God, who is an abyss.
Thus spoke…

April 12, 1968 –
In Kubrick's
Odyssey... A crowd cries: Hey, All Of Us! Long Life to the Renewal of the
Universe! Long Life To Our Endless Life!

May 13, 1882 –
The three Demons, angels, or perhaps just plain folks:

FRITZ, LUIZA, and PAUL...

God is Dead in the minds of these three,
Who freely run, leap,
Jump Up and Down – no moral doubt,
No ambiguity,
No possible punishment –
They are at one together in Love,
Three Persons in spiritual liberty
Beneath the clear, empty
Heavens of late Nineteenth-century Europe, so repressive...

LUIZA:
I am a woman! A virgin!
I am twenty-one!
Males, stand in line!
Leap up and down...
To the tune of our truth! Fritz's nihilism
Invents something for us to aim at...

FRITZ:

Don't talk so much like a woman!
Concern yourself with poetry and silence!
I have had *The Hymn to Life* set to music!

Whoever finds meaning in the last words of this poem
Will know that pain is no impediment to life...

LUIZA:

This is no secret. I know this already, Fritz –

If you have no more happiness to give me,
Well then! You still have your suffering...
Give me your pain...

FRITZ:

Perhaps my music, too, will attain greatness during this moment...
Dreams are the royal road to the unconscious.
There are no facts, only interpretations.

God is dead
In the Galactic darkness, in the Torricelli Void –
Fritz, Luisa, and Paul (like all of us) live...
In an uncontrolled absolute Nothingness,

In the Eternal City,
They, the holy have,
Opened a New World –

Discovering a land of illusionary Hills
In a land where God has
On a rainy afternoon long since given up the ghost –
Some Two Thousand years ago
On a rainy afternoon
By Crucifixion, among wild folk
Jesus died on a Friday –

April 3, 33 AD –
Children say that people have been hanged
For speaking the truth!

Jeanne d'Arc, on fire, at the stake, cried out,
As an answer to what was coming, our time –
God's dead body is coursing through Heaven,
Limpid and transparent – so that
All of us might see this cruel outrageous world
Through His Nebula...

3.

OH! WHAT IS OUR LIFE? BUT A PLAY?
We say – Life is a Game – a GAMBLE –
Fritz Zarathustra – our HERO – says:

Life is the return on an investment in life...

January 10, 2015 –
I am in Las Vegas... Reminding myself why?
This book is called Gambling!
Monte Carlo is the Hotel – after taking
An almost empty air-conditioned shuttle bus
From the Las Vegas Airport, I am standing
Feeling abandoned in this crazy Casino.

"I am a Texan" – this shuttle lady talks to
Me, openly excited –
"I take every vacation at this here Casino, this is where I rest up!
My husband gives me money. To calm things down between us.
He plays cards, craps is my only passion.

"You're Russian? From Moscow? From Toronto? Oh!
We are from Texas! I am John... University at Austin!
You know your Shostakovich if you are Russian...?
I am teaching my students to play his Quartets!
Really? Did you see him when he was alive?
How did he look? Piqued? He slept? Geniuses are strange!

Vladimir! Hey, boy! Come to Texas! We will show you
Where Bush lives – My wife Ellen's a helluva driver!
She cooks good, too…"

4.

Coming out of my modest eleventh-floor bathroom,
I dove into the main-floor ocean,
The neon CASINO crowd...
A burning desert of burning electronic signs,
Between green baize tables, dealers, croupiers, hustlers,
Who are they? So many are young,
Ripe pickings for the mendacity of Mephistopheles...

I do not find Pushkin's
Old Countess singing her aria at a green table,
The Queen of Spades is absent – oh, noble singer of Tchaikovsky's
Gambler with her three Magic Cards –
Maria Philipovna out of Dostoyevsky

There are no mad lovers of money here, but no German
Named Herman (Pushkin
Is not to be found
No Alexey Ivanovich with his Polina –
And Dostoyevsky must be out to lunch in the fluorescent sleaze
Light of a lonely latté at Starbucks
Dostoyevsky belongs here:
Vegas is his kind of territory

5.

Okay okay okay! God is dead –
Fritz has told them so,

She – Lou (also Luiza Gustavovna in Russian) Salomé –
Later – Frau Von Salomé – and later –
After her marriage Andreas-Salomé,
Who had left St. Petersburg, brought by her mother to Rome – where,
At a literary salon, she'd met the attractive gambler and scientist,
Paul Rée – he was a friend of Friedrich Nietzsche's...
Is this young man a Philosopher?
Yes! but not a metaphysician... He is a realist –
Fritz called him *Ree-alist* – "Paul, try enjoying reality," his very words:
"All moral phenomena come from our nature..."

6.

On the Vegas Boulevard,
I met them! ALL THREE PERSONS!
For several hours, I'd hidden in my
Cozy room in the Hotel Monte Carlo Casino and Resort
But then, we'd met for lunch, uttered our respects, and then I'd set them
Free to walk into this world without me,
Free from having to be witnesses...

LUIZA:
Paul, enough of your love aria! We are
Submissively adopting your Postulate,
Together we recognize the crisis inherent in God's death!

FRITZ:
Thanks, Lou!
But be careful, dear girl –

It is not enough to possess talent:
One must also possess permission to possess it –
Eh, my friends?

LUIZA:
Oh, yes! We have talent – all of us!
Maybe not so big as yours! But through all those years...
We have stuck together because of our talent!
On the sidewalk of Rome – of Lucerne,
Or Berlin...

We have been happy –
God is dead but our Holy Trinity lives –
I pray, being Russian Orthodox:

In the Name of the Father,
And of the Son, and of the Holy Ghost… Amen…

Do not laugh, Fritz –
You are our Godfather, and Paul is your Godson –
I am your holy Spirit!

FRITZ:
Dead are all gods: now
We want the Superman to live –
At high noon, let this be our last will.

But that is not der Ubermensch overcoming all Devils…
My Supermen are only ideational!

LUIZA:
Fritz! None of that superman stuff today!
Time doesn't stand still!
It will become the German fashion soon enough
After your death, poor Fritz,
When Elisabeth will pin you to a Nazi flag!

7.

PAUL:
Don't scare us, woman!

LUIZA:
Do you remember that photo,
Taken in Lucerne? I am standing on a cart.
I am smiling, holding a whip...
You are my boys! My horses!
You, Fritz, and you, Paul!
My bit between your teeth.
Horses, horses, horses!

FRITZ:
I witnessed the whipping
Of a horse while travelling to Turin.
I cried... I cannot bear such violence!
I tossed my arms around the horse's holy neck
I collapsed to the ground... Fainted...

LUIZA:
Nothing new about you!
I guess you are my primary patient!
Which is why I will introduce you to
To my friend Josef, author of
A new approach – Psychoanalysis!
He is the first Psychoanalyst –
Sigmund Freud became his young disciple, his protégé.

Both are my friend! So I, Lou Salomé,
Promise you, my Madman Fritz, you will be healed!...
It will happen at Clinic!
Oh, my creative fool, you will compose more melodies
You will be yourself again!
I will translate Russian poems for you,
Turn them into songs –
Warm your blood again.
I will be beside you,
Living in Germany, I now believe I am a German woman –
I am VON Salomé! Still, you are to
Write a Russian romance. Remember?
I read you the poetry of Pushkin for a whole night –
"Incantation" – "Beschwörung" –
Remember? Sing for me now!

FRITZ:
Don't lie! I wrote that when I was twenty!
You, Von Salomé, did not exist!

PAUL:
(Laughing...)

FRITZ:
I remember our Pushkin night –
Paul can confirm though he slept through it all...

Without Music life might be a mistake...

You are right, my foolish Lou…
Sing along with me:

> Oh, if it's true, that in the night
> All have rest who are alive,
> The sky rays of the moon arrive
> At gravestones, a glancing light.
>
> If it's true, we are all from our graves
> Washed away by the storm's waves,
> A sea nymph's briny and becomes foam –
> It's yours – Laila! To freely roam!
>
> Undead, rise up from death, friend,
> And share again in our farewell.
> Pale, cold. Your life has met its end,
> You foresee an inevitable hell.

LUIZA:
I prefer these two heartfelt stanzas –
I will sing:

> You can come like a distant star,
> Or an idyllic music, or a sea breeze.
> Or even – the terrifying ghost – you are –
> Come anyway! Your shade I'll seize!
>
> I shall see you – but not to blame
> Your torturers, who crucified your soul,

No — I do not condemn all of them:
A coffin's mystery is not my goal.

FRITZ (singing):
When my doubts appear some day,
And I'm lost, so — anyway — my wish to say:
I'm yours... Love is alive until today!
Oh, Laila! Come to me! to me! I pray...

Love is immortal. Pushkin knew this...

8.

PAUL:
Who is this beautiful Laila?
Some Persian or Russian Goddess?
If she is Persian, I remember
Only Saadi's Ahurani…
Lou? How about a Russian explanation –

LUIZA:
Calm down Paul… Listen:
Remember Pushkin…
During his Southern exile – he fell for a seductive girl,
A Greek – Calypso Polichroni –
A vibrant woman who died young –
Pushkin was a rake, a trip here, and a trip there…
His wife Natalie, his
"One hundred and thirteenth" love! Yes!

PAUL:
I like it! I like it!

What is our Life?!

LUIZA:
By the way, the name CALYPSO…
Remember the Homeric Calypso!

FRITZ:
Love love love! Each angelic sinless self!
We possess inexhaustible love!
Tell me, my crazy intellectual animals!
Are we happy? Yes? Okay – but
Your Russian Feodor Dostoyevsky
Is closer to the truth, his cry: Love is hell!
Love is a lost Gamble!
God betrothed DEATH to LOVE!

LUIZA:
My dears!
Love is hell…
Pushkin knew all about that!
I told you, he was manly
Among men! Bordering on madness…
He'd lose his mind in love!
Let me read you his heart-
Wrenching confession – how he feared
A whirlygig tilt to his brain.
This poem from between 1830 and 1835
Has its political implications…
This is all so complex… Listen:

> *Lord, I don't want to go insane.*
> *Let me not take Thy name in vain,*
>   *Reduce me not to acedia.*
> *Let hunger deduce only strength from my pain*
> *Yes – yes, I know – I'm barely sane –*
>   *Madness is my middle name:*

Absolve me of my self-abuse!
Give me freedom! – willful, obtuse,
I will climb among tall trees!
Bring morbidity to its knees!
Sing of fire at the heart of ease!
Let me live in dreamland, please.

Let the word insane be left unsaid?
Heaven's abyss hangs overhead
Compelling me to plough the lees…
Or, fell the forest of its trees…
Or, hear how still the sea can be…
Or, simply see what's left to see.

Usually I turn bellicose!
Haggard, so stricken, so morose!
Locked up. Chained. Left for dead.
Not like a man but a dog instead,
Stale crusts fed through an iron slot,
Scrawny treadmill rats share my lot!

Into this sleepless indigo night,
Unlike me, birds swoop in free flight.
Wind-blown trees gather in the asylum yard…
Unruly inmates are in the ward,
Hear their fear, their cries, the clunk
Of leg irons – night nurses drunk…

9.

June 8, 1880 –
Fyodor Mikhailovich made a speech, now famous:

Pushkin's coming aids us mightily in our dark journey by becoming a new guiding light.
Pushkin is presage and prophecy.

LUIZA:
Thank you, Fritz…

FRITZ:
And Pushkin was – please don't laugh – so close to my sense of
Zarathustra: his light sunny poetry, his mutinous
Inner life, his unbridled love
Of Freedom, his faithful love of the Folk –
Anti all absolution
Through object abnegation.
Churches, priests, the psalm's blind
Prayers – were an invitation to satire…

PAUL:
Both of you are Russian Apologists!
We are the German people
With our German culture! Even Lou is now
VON SALOMÉ!

LUIZA:

Yes, I became German. But you are too
Passionate.
I love you very much, my sweet German Boy
With your Jewish blood –
Especially today when I am dying in this our –
Germany, where it is said that there is to be
A new life – with Nazi-installed mousetraps
For ordinary people whose GOD is not dead,
The mob who try to live as best they can, by believing!

10.

LUIZA: *A FINAL MONOLOGUE:*

Readers! Listen to my
Last lecture!
As I began my professional scientific career – beginning
As a follower of Sigmund Freud – so many
Lectures, speeches, presentations…
I now begin on
25 August, 1900!
With a new Millennium opening its shark-like mouth:
My best friend, Fritz,
Joined his dead God…the launching of
Several griefs…

And once you are awake,
You shall remain awake eternally.

Our soulmate
Paul Ludwig Carl Heinrich Rèe passed away…
28 October, 1901.

Zarathustra's words:

Become who you are!
There is more wisdom in your body
Than in your deepest philosophy.

He'd met with his loving friend Fritz in the
Swiss Alps – near Lake Alpsee –
Where The Fairy Tale King Ludwig built
The Neuschwanstein Castle – so Tannhäuser and Lohengrin
Could be performed,
Where Peter Tchaikovsky began to work on *Swan Lake*,
Tchaikovsky rowing on the waters with…
Paul, intending to die? Suicide? Who knows?
Calypso song by Pushkin –
Fritz's *Hymn to Life*!
The sacred ladder – is it going down or is it going up to heaven?
Wherever heaven might be.
Gone to God, who'd also died…
Cinematic shots, lightning flashes, klieg lights…

What then? Sarajevo?

28 June, 1914 –
A single shot in Sarajevo – World War One –
Simple! Chemical warfare became
A major component of global Blitz.
More and more and more
Technology –
Enough!
All about us –
Like blind insects – no goal, no aim, no target, no hope…
Flying, dying,
In our Heaven declared beneath Heaven.
Burying Earth so deep –

By trying to avoid Hell!
We crawl seeking...
Ending up with so much less...
As we see the END...
I am ready to join Fritz's dead God, too,
And both my friends –
But I am still alive
No metaphors from my subconscious as
Herr Freud had taught me –
No, I dream my actual LIFE!
Where nobody's left... So, I will tell you,
My reader,
What I went through on this night in my subconscious,
Me, an old woman
Try to be tolerant, accepting,
See me smile? The smile of a young woman?
Lou von Salomé – who became Andreas-Salomé –
My husband! I whisper to you, dear reader...
Be fleet of foot! In a couple of days I must die...
Are you ready?

31 December, 1937 – (my final nighttime dream):
A logical recurrence out of my brief Past, moving into my endless
Future via my timeless
Presence in the Present...have you been to Venice?
I hope – You can imagine – in the shadows of a
Romanesque wall of old stones...

11.

A FINAL VENICE DREAM, A Long Monologue:

*We go to Basilica St. Louis, to Wilmot Street where high walls narrow the
sidewalk passages... I am happy with my husband who renamed me –
"Andreas"! I am happy strolling... DO YOU KNOW? This "deck" is
made of Russian trees – this mystic floor in VENICE. It's not land! It's a
FERRY! A Russian Ferry from Siberia! My feet feel light of foot...*

*"Carl! My loving husband! We are high-stepping through Siberia –
enjoying Venice! Oh, my German Ignoramus! My fool, my loving
husband! Listen to the trembling sound, the Sad Russian Cry of jailed
orphans... Our fantastic Odyssey on the Siberian river, Enisei! These
mad logs were alive for 700 Years!..."*

Then – THEN – 11 April, 1899 – (Real Time in Venice)
   *"Young man! Do you know you are in Siberia? Stop reading! Please
be polite – Show some respect for a lady! Answer me! Don't be afraid! I
am a kind woman, a German-Russian Frau! Strolling through Siberia in
Venice...*
   *And I see – Carl steps back into the shadows to lean against a stone
wall, to smoke a cigar... He knows I have the psychologist's habit of
talking to strangers... His smoke is blowing on my face. I am moving closer
to a young man who is reading a German book, he is sitting on a stone
bench...*
   *Remember! I made him mine in Venice in 1887. He was so complaisant,
this twenty-one-year-old young poet. I was thirty-three. We walked close to
each other. Carl Andreas followed behind. A narrow passage between walls,*

deep dark shadows under arches. The ravaged limestone of the old Romanesque
walls betrayed sunlight. The imperceptible breathing of the ancient floor of
Venice. Siberian Larches are Venice at its base, a foundation. They can live for
700 years. Alas, this "ferry" is suffering from too many people on the chaotic
move, sinking peacefully. The gondoliers' oars flash through this solemnity...

Rilke waited for me, he became RAINER instead of his given name, René.
He was so young, so attractive, timid, and so masochistic...
    "I am nobody. Who are you?"

I remember a Kremlin Easter celebration:
Plump apple, smooth banana, melon, peach,
Gooseberry... How all this affluence
Speaks of death and life in the mouth... I sense...
Observe it in a child's transparent features...

My new friend Rilke! I told him:
"You shall be called RAINER! I do not like René..."
Accepting his new name.
He kissed me passionately!
And we were together until his death...
"Your love is warm" — I told him — his wish was
To be as close to me as possible! And these are my words to him
(Alas, only after death...):

    If for years I was your woman,
    It was because you were for me
    The first real truth —
    Undeniable proof of life itself.

Word for word, I could have repeated to you
What you said to me as a confession of love:
"You alone are real to me."
With these words we were wed,
Before we had even become friends...
Two halves did not seek completion in each other.
But a surprised whole recognized itself
In an unfathomable totality
Come the first day, arise we from
God's very hand wherein we've slept
For how long,
I could not tell. The present's past
Is still at zero. Time, begin!

My Rainer! Study Russian, my mother language! Go to Tolstoy who is still Alive! Read Pushkin! My Maria Rainer Rilke kissed me – and recited his poems to me in his baritone:

And which violinist holds us in his hand?

May – August 1900 –
Rainer's itinerary: Moscow, Tula, Leo Tolstoy's estate at Yasnaya Polyana, Kiev, Kremenchug, Poltava, Kharkov, Voronezh, Saratov, Simbirsk, Kazan, Nizhny Novgorod, Yaroslavl, and back to Moscow.

He was fascinated by Russian Orthodoxy, Russian spirituality appealed to him – he partook in the Easter celebrations at the Kremlin, etched in his memo...

12.

I am approaching my most significant goal –
I was always a follower of Sigmund Freud
And now, in my seventies –
I am a real PSYCHOANALYST…

Do you remember Fritz's horses?
His mad illusion that the Horse is a pert-minded
Gentleman? His kissing the horses' faces?
He was serious!
There was a time I brought him to Freud's teacher –
Doctor Josef Breuer and together we helped him…
We handed him back to the world who read him passionately –
Who loved his talent, his intellect, his aesthetic soul…

After that – in his head – he had no HORSES, no migraines –
Fritz had embraced
Zarathustra and Zarathustra embraced him
In the cosmic thunderstorm.
Poor Fritz –
He ended his life in the Mad House.

The heavy iron Bell chimes
For the funereal World of the Thirties!
Hitler's campfires burn books, German geniuses!
While the greatest crime in Hitler's books was to be of Jewish blood!

No Freud... No Breuer...

Russian Communists joined
German Fascists... Diplomatically...
In the Russian cradle – St. Petersburg:

Akhmatova stood in a long long line before the jail!
Hoping to give a parcel to her innocent son!

> *I never sought asylum among aliens*
> *Never cowled myself in a crow's wings.*
> *I stood as my people stood, alone –*
> *In my marrowbones, their sorrow.*

Poor Akhmatova... She didn't believe Fritz –
She was so Russian!
She believed only in her Russian Christ, a Christ surrounded by
Jewish friends –
Kneeling in tears, the Church helping her to survive...

> *Angels in their grief are moaning.*
> *Heaven is on fire and melting.*
> *Unto the Father: "Why hast Thou forsaken...?"*
> *And to the Mother: "Weep no more."*

I realize my God is dead – He couldn't help me:
My holy work, crushed!
My memorabilia, all the books – Breuer, Freud, my many

Co-scientists, thinkers destroyed!
Yes, it had begun and has continued long past the bloody Thirties…
Tears pour down my wrinkled cheeks!
Remember:
I was a Russian beauty at twenty-one when I went out into the
Great European World…
Now, I am a prominent scientist, but I am so sick, so old –
I am crawling into my eighties…

13.

Attacked by Nazi interrogators:
"HELLO! Are you Frau Andreas-Salomé?
You are a Jewess, we found evidence!
You are an intimate accomplice of the alchemist,
That charlatan – that so called world-renowned scientist –
Sigmund Freud! His appearance
In the list of your crimes is huge!
You are culpable! Your sentence:
Jail! Concentration Camp! Or simply – to be shot!
Why did you breed conflict
Between Herr Neitzsche
And his honest sister, Elisabeth, Nazi supporter and
A faithful patriot!
You are not a German woman!
You are... You are... You are..."

Please stop!
My Germany is Beethoven!
Heinrich Heine and Johann Goethe!
Dürer and Holbein and Emil Nolde,
Max Ernst, Paul Klee and Kandinsky!
And how about Meister Gutenberg!

I am not a Jewish woman! But I am close,
In our Christian Country, to a Jewish man!
You are all Christians!
Aryan men, Germans!

A Jewish God did not die for you! He is with you –
The JEWISH GERMAN JESUS is alive.
Perhaps what I have to say is merely metaphorical, a poetical cry…
Not even close to Fritz's meaning…
But metaphorically I am saying
That I am now actually standing on Golgotha, near our Christ…
His neighbours – two sad thieves, two saints – as I transform into a
Sick old scientific woman – Andreas-Salomé –

You are right – near Him I am a Jewish woman –
My parents, however, were actually French Huguenots
Of northern German descent…
So I am who I am here… But on the Cross I am a
Jewish woman… And you – Adolf Hitler's officers –
Leave me alone to die peacefully in my own bed…

No jail… No camp… No firing squad… It is late…
My dressed coffin waits for me, for its natural, noble use…
My library that I love is obliterated…
My fellow scientists are a lonely crowd in HELL…
Tears pour down my wrinkled cheeks!

Time has Chimed! I Close My Eyes –
In Göttingen…in my Germany… In Lower Saxony…

The River Leine runs through our city washing clear
The people's blood…
Also my death… The death of all the Russians, Germans, Orthodox
(What do I mean – a Jewish Woman on Golgotha) – Lou's Salomé…?

120

My dream is that my coffin might be drowned
In the Neva in St. Petersburg... My dream died in 1917...

5 February, 1937 –
Goodbye... Auf Wiedersehen... o   ...

In the Name of the Father, and of the Son, and of the Holy Ghost...

FRITZ:
Amen...

PAUL:
Amen...

ON "THE DEATH OF IVAN ILYICH"

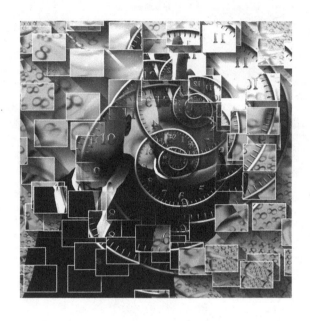

*Suddenly some force struck him in the chest and side,
making it still harder to breathe, and he fell through the hole
and there at the bottom was a light…*

—LEO TOLSTOY. *The Death of Ivan Ilyich*

Why am I, an author, Vladimir Pavlovich, fixated on Leo Tolstoy? Why am I going to focus on one of his greatest stories to tell this one? Simple. This is my story. It shares the same title as his story and some of the names, but what you read here is really about me. I have unabashedly used Tolstoy's title to attract readers to my story. So, if you are reading this, my design, my storytelling architecture, has worked. I cannot apologize for this.

I have written by myself for myself. I did not have a stenographer as Tolstoy did in his wife, Sofia Andreevna. His novella is partly about him. Mine, as I said, is partly about me. Consider this story to be my sequel to his in which love and death called to me and asked me to leave my T-square and drafting board for the rhythmic seclusion of a typewriter. I like to think that in his search for his character he found some part of me. I am simply returning the favour as best I can by finding a design in the life I once lived that helped me to find him.

It is a well-known fact that Tolstoy was not alone in creating his characters and their world. Starting with *War and Peace*, his diarist spouse also offered her strong, principled, intellectual opinion. I admire her work, and I think that writers should either keep a diary or examine life as a series of entries or stories that captured the moments when love and death transformed them. Between Tolstoy and his Sofia Andreevna, everything was an exact argument. She had her suggestions: make *it* stronger, smarter, throw *it* away! Their emotional alliance survived several battles, their lives were a rough coastline with tides and ebb tides... Me? I am alone, alone...

I have no creative dialogues. I just hear my characters' conversations, as if they are not dead... I am still in love with the moment: They speak to me as I sit at my typewriter. They follow me through my days, stand in my room as I sleep, come to me in my dreams.

In one of my dreams, I called: "Please! Sofia Andreevna! Great moralist and critic! Great stenographer! Help me with my work!"

She came to me, telling me: "Vladimir, I am glad you are trying to help my Leo become contemporary. Heaven knows he could use a change of idiom. But, Vladimir, you've got to realize that readers are very different today. People, not only architects like you, but all Muscovites, all Russians, are in need of some kind of explanation. Who is who, what is what? Life today is, well, so prosaic, to say nothing of literature. Everyone wants a quick fix...'this happened, then that happened.' No one's got time to read an epic."

"Thank you for your helpful words!"

"No, thank you, Vladimir! I'll tell my husband what you intend the next time I see him. Now, I will read your little masterpiece and enjoy it, as if I knew you in your Russia back in the Seventies. My Leo may not need your tribute to his great work, but I suspect he will thank you for making his name live again in that particular space and time."

I

The morning rush-hour Moscow Metro is crowded. Vladimir Pavlovich is about to be late for his job. He can't board the third train. Crowded. Crazy Moscow! How many millions live here now? Every year the number swells... The train door is in front of him.

He pushes ahead of a lady who has two huge bags. She trips on the threshold to the door. He sighs deeply, satisfied. Elbow-to-elbow. Then, the monotonous shaking.

Several stops flash by. Not too many more – two, three... Swaying, he yields to the rhythm of the train, trying to relax before work.

What?

Vladimir Pavlovich catches sight of a familiar face. Someone he knows in this crazy crowd! How often does that happen? Vladimir Pavlovich knows him! Yes, his former colleague, a young architect.

A sudden recollection! Peter! From the notorious Studio 20! Yes! Vladimir Pavlovich calls out through the Metro's noise:

"Nice to see you, Peter!"

"Vladimir Pavlovich! Glad to run into you!"

"Haven't seen you in ages! I'm on my way to visit my old office. What's that...about Ivan Ilyich? It's so noisy!"

"You've got an important visit to make, Vladimir Pavlovich, to see your architect friend, architect Ivan Ilyich Golovin!"

"What about him?"

"His sixtieth. Today's his birthday. The party's next week. I saw your name on the invitation list."

"Is he okay? I remember he was ill. Couldn't visit our last architects' get-together at the Soyuz Club."

"He wasn't well for a while, now he's okay…"

"I am so glad…"

"Sorry, my stop! See you soon, Vladimir Pavlovich!"

Vladimir Pavlovich is alone, sardined into the crowd. Unsettling thoughts rush through his mind about his old job. Such a creative time. He misses it. The lost happiness of creative life. Yes, as he utters the name – Ivan Ilyich…

Ivan Ilyich! One of his friends back then, and now he's his adversary… An enemy? No! It's not that easy. They had a great connection for years before the incident at work. No, he is not an enemy! Vladimir Pavlovich remembers Ivan Ilyich's words when they worked together:

"Vladimir! Your artistic, your architectural taste, is beyond reproach!"

He'd heard this so often from the esteemed Ivan Ilyich, but then Ivan Ilyich had slammed the Studio 20 door on him! Ivan Ilyich! So stubborn, so uncompromising. That's what Vladimir Pavlovich had loved about Ivan Ilyich, his pig-headedness… Someone from the old Soviet regime… Sixty now?

His name, like an incantation. Ivan Ilyich? Ivan Ilyich!…

Oh, wild memory! Vladimir Pavlovich's rising voice among the commuters:

"Tolstoy's story: *The Death of Ivan Ilyich*!

A coincidence? He remembers the Tolstoy book, small, a green cover. A novella. Sitting on a shelf alongside all his Tolstoy books, but somehow separate, *The Death*… He should read it again, after work tonight. But why does the name and the idea of reading the book excite him? And why does the name of his co-worker make him so nervous?

In the train window, Vladimir Pavlovich sees his own tightly-drawn face. He's trying to figure out what's happened to him... The train's rhythmic shaking slows. He has reached his station. The last shudder of the metal floor beneath his feet. Elbowing with all his strength, he moves through the unyielding crowd.

Breathes the fresh June air. The gentle morning sun. Hurry. Almost 9:30... The Metro encounter, stuck in his mind. He looks ahead, imagines his working day. His repellent job. Already unbearable! How can he get out of his boring occupation?

His watch: 10:30. Two blocks more. Arriving a little later than usual. He needs a more flexible schedule.

"Every morning, I go to my job just to check, correct and confirm the mountain of boring blueprints! If I had free time during the working day, I could find something better, something more suited to my talents... Yes! But what, and how?"

At the Research-Project Institute, he pushes the entrance door open. Showing his entry permit, he walks to the elevator, greeting co-workers on the way.

Something sad seizes him:

"What? What's happening in my head?"

He stops in the lobby. Something is crying in him:

"I always drew pictures, architectural sketches! My fountain pen! My pencils. These are the tools I used for *writing*! I have a secret notebook. A diary. Nobody has read it. Not even my wife."

II

Vladimir Pavlovich... Is in the middle of the lobby...

A smiling girl says to him:

"Why are you standing in the lobby, Vladimir Pavlovich?".

"Sorry, sorry... Oh! Hello..." He doesn't remember her name...

He leaps between the closing doors of the elevator. A sudden attack, a blitzkrieg of realization in his mind during his ascent:

"There is a new East-Demographic-German Optima Typewriter in my work room. At home, I have my Moscow typewriter. Not as new. I love my home machine..."

Nobody in the room looks at him as they gather to drink their morning tea. Kind Masha has probably brought a baked sweet pie. Vladimir Pavlovich passes the tea drinkers, steals through the piles of the drawing and tracing-paper rolls, stacks of blueprints and bales of paper sheaths. He reaches his place. A new idea: be a writer! Can he describe what happened in the Metro? "My revolutionary moment! Still fresh. An idea is calling!"

He sees the mountain of papers, his working day: "Later! Later!"

He hears the future clacking on his typewriter... He hears Masha's voice: "One piece or two?"

"No! Later! Later!"

He's at the pristine keyboard. Rests his fingers on the keys. Be aggressive! Fingers fly, hammers strike the roller... Blitzkrieg? Blitzkrieg!

III

Among the many in the crowded rush-hour Moscow Metro, Vladimir Pavlovich catches sight of a familiar face. Yes, that's his former colleague, a young architect. No last name. He can't remember the family name. Vladimir Pavlovich remembers him as just Peter. He cries out through the Metro noise:

"Nice to see you, Peter!"

"Oh, hello, Vladimir Pavlovich!"

"I haven't seen you for a while, but later I will be visiting your office. What'd you say? What about Ivan Ilyich? It's so noisy!"

"Ivan Ilyich Golovin is dead. Two days ago…"

"What?"

"Ivan Ilyich Golovin is dead. Two days ago…"

Vladimir Pavlovich is on the verge of tears! This is so bizarre! His birthday! Freud's proviso! Why in my imagination do I hate him? Deeper? He was the reason I left my job… But he is having a birthday party. I need to greet him! We were friends for years… Vladimir Pavlovich began to write his diary like fiction… And from now on he will write, think, invent…a different direction. "Come back? No? No! Delete the last phrases? No? No!"

Vladimir! Follow your intuition. Tolstoy's rival… But it is impossible. Don't laugh! Smile, be ironic… Slightly wary, cynical… Do not mock the 70s Soviet era… You lived there…

Staring at the Optima typewriter, it's scary…open-mouthed…he whispers the name of Ivan Ilyich…hears the voice of his living machine, his typewriter.

"You are a Writer! Vladimir! Architecture be damned! Let's type! Don't be sorry about the paper! Spoiled. Drafts! Different versions! Try it this way, that! Say something different! Thanks to Khrushchev's Thaw, you know all about the Great Modern Trinity: Proust, Kafka, Joyce! Your job allows you to read what you want in the Lenin Library in Moscow, second largest in the world after the Library of Congress... Banned Russian literature, banned foreign literature... Forge ahead!"

Vladimir Pavlovich whispers: "What did you say?"

"What about Ivan Ilyich?"
"Ivan Ilyich Golovin is dead..."
"Impossible... I saw him..."
"Sorry, my stop. Sorry for our loss...take care, goodbye."

In a loud voice, the Metro announcer summons the door open. Peter elbows his way through the squall of people on the platform, disappears in the multiheaded mass. Vladimir Pavlovich stands alone with this shocking news. Alone in his mind, pressed, pressured by hot bodies...tries moving deeper into the train car, feeling slightly wonky, he lifts his hand, holds onto the warm metal bar. Ivan Ilyich is dead... Ivan Ilyich... He'd seen him recently in the cellar restaurant where architects gather, the Soyuz Club. "Hi!" they'd said to each other, smiling. Ivan Ilyich with his co-workers. Thoughts flashing.

Vladimir Pavlovich stops typing, considers his style, the syntax, punctuation. He sees ellipses...ellipses, not periods... And he remembers – a time long ago when he liked dashes. Yes! Dashes-dashes-dashes— in his amateur poems. Following on the heels of Laurence Sterne's *Tristram Shandy*! When he first read Sterne – it was so strange – being a semi-literate lover of literature – Sterne's Eighteenth-century riot of ideas – it seemed so Avant-Garde? He knew that word! During The Thaw – there had been a Russian Avant-Garde! The forgotten, the jailed, the murdered... "We are the happy ones who lived in the 70s..."

Vladimir Pavlovich looks around. He needs a break. Just a short one...He approaches the tea drinkers: "Masha, pour me a tea, too. Thanks... No, just one..." With a tea cup, just like at home! Nobody pays attention to him... He takes a couple of sips of the hot tea.

Then something sharp, new, hot, extraordinary, blows into his mind. A revolution in thought? Writing is not a crime! No, no, no! Certainly not the dream of a man's death! Leo Tolstoy rescued him! This coincidence of *names* pushes him *to follow* the Classics! This book that he hadn't read with enough care...what a disgrace, to have taken it lightly! And now! Now he must go back, must diligently study the masterpiece, *The Death of Ivan Ilyich*! What will he do? Transform it into a different time, different idiom, different characters... Tolstoy's Ivan Ilyich is a "member of the Supreme Court" of Tsarist Russia! Vladimir Pavlovich's hero is I.I. Golovin, citizen of the USSR! That's it!

Typing, typing! (he resisted the idea that he was hallucinating by checking that the keyboard letters were in their natural order...) In his head, something framed. Why no emotional reaction to this death? Colleague, co-worker, and – yes, adversary! That this should happen during a work week! Back! To the Metro... And to them! To his former colleagues! To Studio 20! And then to ask himself: "What more? And more? What next?"

He is on the street. He rushes, runs. To the Metro! To Moscow Centre, take the Metro, transfer to his internal cosmic space, to his working space – inside Mayakovsky Square! This is where his history began, where the entirety of being and of being an architect began... And then, out of tragedy, his break from it all... Thanks to you, Ivan Ilyich!

Again, the wagging wobble of the speeding train car. The same feeling... A bitter taste in his mouth... Pulsing temples... Stuffiness of the summer. It's only early June. Is there air-conditioning in the Moscow Metro? The dark, mirroring window reflects...

A couple of stops more... Hey! Vladimir Pavlovich, can you honestly say what has been born in your brain? Confess, Vladimir. Send out your candid sorrow... Back two stops to his working space! To the Mayakovsky Square... Studio 20...

What station was he at? Which stop? He gets off at the Station of the Revolution. By this time, it is already afternoon. But he needs to go out to breathe before battle! To think, to dream, to breathe... "Okay... It is so simple... I can confess!" This is really simple! Vladimir Pavlovich sees Ivan Ilyich's office. He sees his dead colleague... And then, the room is empty. A legendary chair is unoccupied... *Confess?* His last two structures! *Unfinished!* The cause of his trouble!

Huge crowds, a multiheaded, multilegged mass... People are walking, strolling, talking, laughing, or just silently existing, a moving, nameless animated monster. It was always so in Moscow, particularly near the Kremlin, where there are so many tourists, guests, lovers of the revolutionary Red Square. Some just crave seeing the fantastic multicoloured Saint Basil's Cathedral under the blue, sunny, early summer sky.

Hey... Vladimir Pavlovich... You are in Red Square! Stop your sentimental sorrowing. At least for the moment. When were you here last? Around these amazing ancient stones of Russian history? A year? Two? Sorry, maybe ten!

As an architect, you always felt pride seeing some of the best architecture in the world. Even after your trips to Italy. After Romeo and Juliet's town, Verona, where you were shocked by the red-brick walls – so like the Moscow Kremlin. These magic, sacred red bricks of the Kremlin under the bright sky of Italy! Maybe it was a crime to say that during the Stalinist regime? But it was sublime happiness to see a bit of Russia in Italy! And the towers of the Renaissance in Verona! Like our Kremlin Towers! Their red stars, whirling, leaping from tower to tower to tower!

And the great Soviet architect, icon of Stalin's time, Ivan Zholtovsky... he appeared in Italy... he appeared in Vladimir Pavlovich's imagination! His Smolensky Tower, famous in Moscow. The inspiration for his idea! His, Vladimir Pavlovich's twenty-four-storey building! The district, so distant from the Kremlin... Named a funny old name from hundreds of years ago – Konkovo-Derevlevo!

Vladimir Pavlovich turns his head toward the Kremlin Saviour Tower. He stops for a minute! He hears a great tolling call!

Bong! Bong! Bong!

You remember the name of the Italian master who built this Russian stone beauty, the main Kremlin Tower? Pietro Antonio Solari! Maybe he was from Verona? The style so familiar after the Verona visit... And the same details. The same snaggle teeth around the top of the brick walls!

Vladimir Pavlovich thinks, smiling:

"To your happiness, Italian, Pietro Solari: you came to Russia long before the reign of our Ivan the Terrible (around 1490, as I remember). Thank God, you knew nothing of the destiny of two Russian artists, Barma and Postnik, who were blinded after they designed the fantastic St. Basil's..."

"Never again, nothing like this ever again! Put out their eyes!" Ivan The Terrible had said in his voice incroyable...

Bong! Bong! Bong!

Three hammers knock! Three o'clock! Time to go to Studio 20... You'll be a tad late...

"Hurry, to get in on time for the remainder of the working day! Preserve your mad impetus to write!"

Metro again! Two short stops! The short escalator... Left, then right, up the marble stairs... Run through the square. Vladimir Pavlovich's workspace for many years... The sunny days of early summer, the rising winds. He crosses Mayakovsky Square – Square of the great Soviet poet. Quick steps. So vigorous, so hearty. The rhythm of poetry. Yes, like before, like many years ago! Like the important part of his biography! A poet's life is so complicated, so mad. Politics versus Love... His great poetic lines filled with eternal optimism!

Stars being lit

Means someone needs them.

Someone wants them to be,

> Someone deems those miniscule lights
> Magnificent!

Vladimir Pavlovich pulled open the solid oak door. Showed his still-valid permit card. In the elevator, he smiled, greeting his former colleagues:
    "Hi! I know this is a sad event! Such a terrible loss!"
    He reaches the sixth floor. Studio 20.

V

"Natasha! I hope you remember this escaped architect. I hope we're still friends. I'd like to see Mikhail Semenovich. I'll just be a couple of minutes…"

"Hello, Vladimir Pavlovich. So nice to see you. Of course, we are friends! Sorry, he's in a meeting now. Then he has lunch. Maybe you can join him? Please wait. Or call him tomorrow."

"No, no! I will wait. Such a serious and sad moment. I should talk to him. Why else am I here…?"

Vladimir Pavlovich closes the door. Such an inauspicious beginning. Vladimir Pavlovich is in the corridor. His colleagues move around him and pass him by.

"Yes. Hi. Hi. And hi! Yes. And yes… I heard the sad news. It is so sad…"

Leaning against the corridor wall, drenched in memories, Vladimir Pavlovich comes back to his new, difficult thought… He has doubts.

"To run or not to run. But, the King is absent now… I have time to think… Maybe time to rehearse an impending, unpleasant conversation…" The chair… He's sitting…

Memories flood his mind, stealing Vladimir Pavlovich's attention. His thoughts turn to an unforgettable moment at the Arch-Council meeting. The official meeting of this bloated building project organization! He remembers Ivan Ilyich's brave speech in defence of his Vladimir Pavlovich, towered (yes precisely, Towered) Konkovo-Derevlevo! With an outstretched hand, he had pointed to the plans like he was Lenin in bronze, Lenin pointing, always pointing.

"We need to save this Soviet era Architectural statement! We need it! I say we need it! As an echo of our Fifties genius, Zholtovsky! And we must heed the brave call of our young architect, Vladimir Pavlovich!"

A second architectural dream, the Youth Palace! Closer than Konkovo, much closer, on the Sadovaya Ring, a singular, non-industrial public building. A project ready to begin construction. But now – there are just the concrete ramps… Monolithic concrete… The exterior was to be glass, glass, glass! Oh, the craziness of it. Once, in a dream, I realized that my great temple needed a more monumental entrance! Some inviting stylobate! The God of Architecture whispered to Vladimir Pavlovich, "Add one more level!" It is possible! Just fight! Be stubborn!

After the sharp rejection of that project, Vladimir Pavlovich left Studio 20…

Vladimir Pavlovich checks the time. He has waited more than thirty minutes and he's tired of sitting. Changing position, he opens a notebook. He has an idea for a fragment of a story about those two buildings. And how he waited for his former, perhaps future, boss.

Unexpectedly, the elevator door slides open. Mikhail Semenovich's solid figure enters the hallway leading to his office. Noticing his visitor, he offers an interested but puzzled smile…

Vladimir Pavlovich leaps up from the chair:

"Hello Mikhail Semenovich!"

Mikhail Semenovich is surprised, but responds evenly:

"Is that you? You are here? Come in, come in, Pavlovich! Natasha, I am with a guest. Please, two teas for us. Sit down, feel free."

VI

"*You have his portrait on the wall! Our Ivan Vladislavovich.*"

"*I always respected Zholtovsky. But after your twenty-four floor complex, your precious baby, your Konkovo-Derevlevo, with it's rotunda-crown like Zholtovsky's Moscow building for the Soviet élites – I ran into problems because of your bravery, the Renaissance style Zholtovsky had injected into that Stalinist Epoch when we were in the grip of Gulag culture, when all the revolutionary architecture of the past deteriorated into wreckage, all failed! My God, just a couple of Art Deco buildings put up to tease us, the scent of the Capitalist West stuffed up the noses of our leaders...*"

"*Mikhail Semenovich...*"

"*I certainly held Zholtovsky in high regard. His pretending that he'd forgotten all our revolutionary avant-garde achievements – trying in spite of everything to give our Soviet gods something human in the form of architecture, tried to draw them away from ideological and political terrorism...*"

"*That swarm of bees were all around us all the time. Now, too. We can be stung...*"

"*I like your tone. You are still a new voice, Pavlovich! Bravo!*"

"*No, it's just I'm inspired and saddened by my friend Ivan Ilyich.*"

"*I thought you came to share our grief. But I can guess why you are really here.*"

"*I saw Zholtovsky on your wall. It was so exciting for me to recall the love Ivan Ilyich had for him. My Konkovo-Derevlevo project was rescued by Ivan Ilyich...and for both of us, our inspiration was Zholtovsky! His Solensky building.*"

"Vladimir, it's done. And are you happy?"

"I went to Ivan Ilyich, and asked if I could renovate our Youth Palace!"

"Oh, my God! Nobody wanted to let you touch the second floor! You know that. You've come a long way since then."

"Let me finish my work. I've lost my friend and mentor, I want to finish what I started."

"Just come to the funeral! Hey Natasha!"

"He is alive for me…"

"Yes, yes! He's at the morgue! You are absolutely crazy. I remember you don't smoke…but let me show you…this is a gift from a German Company."

"Sorry, I don't!"

"No, not for you. When we were young Ivan Ilyich and I smoked together. It was difficult to find a place to smoke. We smoked in the stinking washroom like school boys!"

"Why remember that?"

"A couple of days ago, we completed a renovation – a special smoking room with expensive German equipment! Great ventilation! It's a big money deal to make our Institute more modern. Big money! A new lifestyle for us. Our girls want to be like the Hollywood Stars of the Thirties."

"Don't show me a new interior. It is strange enough to be back here even though I am the same. Today, it seems, nothing has changed!"

"Today? Today's a very gloomy, rainy day."

"Today is a June day. Beneath a big, bright, Moscow sky!"

"Yes, June 14, 1975. Just two days since Ivan Ilyich's death. There is his comfy leather chair, which he bought with his own money. Still warm after his ass has gone cold"

"Ivan Ilyich! May he rest in peace… We are alive."

"*You make me wary. You won't understand the Youth Palace! We're already at the second floor! You look exhausted! Go home! Sleep, Pavlovich!*"

"*Mikhail Semenovich! My Uncle Sam! I feel naked, abandoned in the world without Ivan Ilyich.*"

"*Maybe you need a little funeral food, vodka in his memory?*"

"*Don't mock me...*"

"*No...!*"

"*I am... I am your honest servant! Maybe the first and best!*"

"*You're pushing your luck! Natasha, see our man off! Call Lubov Arkadievna!*"

Ivan Ilyich died in hospital in the Baumanovsky District, east of Moscow. Two days ago, after a week in the intensive care ward. Three weeks before, he was lying on his sofa, bedridden at home. His kidneys failed. For many years, he'd suffered the symptoms. He'd gone through serious treatments. Urinalysis, ultrasounds, angiograms – all routine, until the last bout when his kidneys went into total renal failure. In the early morning when he was on his way to work. The emergency ward doctor suggested that he should be at home. No work. So, he went home. Alone. He phoned his friends. Called about projects on the go. His wife, Praskovia Fedorovna, called, asking if he needed her help. He did not. His nephew, a foster son, Gerasim, tried to help him. And when Ivan Ilyich's condition worsened, Gerasim was there for him every afternoon. The young man was quick and handy and fed his uncle, sitting beside him on the sofa. Ivan Ilyich was happy with this. Ivan Ilyich went downhill quickly. Gerasim tended to him every afternoon. The Boss told him his being sick would be treated like vacation time.

Vladimir Pavlovich thinks that it is better to describe what Tolstoy's novella says in its most psychological, painful flights into the cosmos. He is not Tolstoy. He is at home, at his desk. With great sadness, Tolstoy's novella awaits rereading:

> When I am not, what will there be? There will be nothing. Then where shall I be when I am no more? Can this be dying? No, I don't want to! He jumped up and tried to light the candle, felt

for it with trembling hands, dropped both candle and candle-
stick on the floor, and fell back on the pillow. "What's the use?
It makes no difference," he said to himself, staring with wide-
open eyes into the darkness. "Death. Yes, death."

No. The dying Soviet architect is much happier. His Gerasim is not a
serf, a servant of the semi-rich from pre-revolutionary Russia. No. Gerasim
is a nephew, a close young friend.

As he lay on the sofa, Ivan Ilyich said to Gerasim.

*"When you are near, Gera, my pain goes away. But my pain is sharper,
constant. I am happy you are here…"*

*"Soup's ready, Ivan Ilyich. Chicken noodle with some veggies. The chicken
is Hungarian. It's okay? And I bought spinach pies at a new café. Yulia's sug-
gestion. Remember her? Our nice waitress? She knows you are at home. Take
this piece of pie. Eat it with the soup…"*

"Gera, these are all so delicious. Thank you, dear…"

"You okay to eat now?"

"Yes, dear. I feel I'm hungry. I need to eat. Thank you, Gerasim…"

*"The sofa, you can't lie on the sofa for a whole day. Ivan Ilyich, you need
assistance."*

*"I am much better now. And I have this hellish need to share with you
what's going on with my kidneys… You hear me? You are so tolerant, poor
boy."*

"Ivan Ilyich! Your story needs ears."

*"About food. I have lots of funny stories… I remember a couple of years
ago, my appointment with the Main Moscow Urologist."*

"That wasn't easy to get!"

"Right! What a woman! She looked like Catherine the Great! Ella Eduardovna! She stared into my soul! Her words were magic: 'Metabolism, metabolism, this is reason enough…'"

"You're so funny…"

"She made a pronouncement, a treatment plan, in her measured tone: 'A paradoxical diet for Russians who are not alcoholics. And you are not one. So, fifty grams of vodka before breakfast, for seven days! No Stolichnaya, you need Moskovskaya – the bottle with the green label. Good luck!'"

"What? Is that a joke?"

"It's the truth, absolutely…"

"Okay…"

"Imagine – after my morning vodka, I'd go to my job! Young Natasha had just started working at Studio 20… She was afraid of me, reeking of morning drink… Sorry… This ache in my lower back! Please, dear boy, rub it… Lightly… Yes, like that… And take your soup away…"

"Lie on your stomach…"

"Okay, I'll try. You're the best doctor, Gera. I am almost okay… So, this woman was so elegant and beautiful…"

"Who?"

"Ella Eduardovna. With her mad diet. Did it help? I don't think so. I met her at the Bolshoi with some strange friends. I greeted her and thanked her. I was well at the time."

"Is there something you want?"

"Something different… I need the washroom, quickly!"

"Hold on to my neck."

"This must be very unpleasant for you. Forgive me. I am helpless."

"Uncle? I am your caregiver…"

"Stop here, Gera. I'd like to sit a bit on the chair…"

"No problem."

"Listen! This is not about my stupid kidneys. I want to help you, Gera, in no small way."

"What do you mean?"

"See the thick illustrated book on my desk? The big one?"

"What of it?"

"I'm emptying my home these days, there's this volume… Canon of the Five Orders of Architecture by Vignola. It's the textbook on architecture and building. It was a textbook at our Institute. I had a dog-eared copy, very old and tattered. This glossy volume is one I bought a couple of years ago in Italy! You remember what I brought for you?"

"Thank you again, it was such a warm sweater!"

"My heart belongs to Florence where Vignola worked with Michelangelo on the completion of St. Peter's Basilica. Their domes were so similar in design that they must have crowded each other out. Such were the great treasures of the Renaissance! And that is when Michelangelo wrote these words as a poet. He loved poets, passionately, love was king in his heart."

I'll be clear and certain, free of doubt.
If you hide from me, I'll pardon you
When you are out and about
Even if I'm blind, I will find you…

"I've got a pulsing pain…"

"What can I do?"

"Just listen! Be stubborn! Love your life! Go to Italy and study Classical architecture there. I've told you many times. Before your pilgrimage to Italy, explore Vignola's book. Oh my God! Again…"

"*Calm down. Don't talk!*"

"*God, it's so bad. The pain…Please, go to Italy when you get the chance. Understand, Gera? Italy. A builder needs to know the Renaissance. We have money…*"

"*Is it worse?*"

"*Call them.*"

Gerasim calls an ambulance.

"*Gerasim, call Mikhail Semenovich, but don't call Praskovia. Let her find out from the hospital.*"

"*Don't worry*".

"*The Vignola book is on my desk. Bend down. Let me kiss you…*"

VIII

"Give me a cigarette."

"Okay... Yes... To sadness... But you know, Angela, and you, Glafira, one of my friends died three times! Don't laugh. It's true!"

"What do you mean, died three times? What kind of madness is that?"

"It's the truth. Once – it was almost real death. Some sort of clinical death under the knife during heart surgery. The doctor pronounced him dead, and then told his wife who was waiting in the lobby... She fainted...was taken home...her friends and relatives gathered!"

"Okay, but listen – Vera told me Praskovia Fedorovna's already visited him in the morgue... I wonder what she'll wear for her funeral gown? She's a fashionable woman... Maybe that explains their separation."

"No, it was something else! He was a man. She is a woman. Even today, she is attractive. But why didn't they live together? He was such a easy man... Now, his widow will have to look after all the financial matters. She's still his wife with all her elegance. They weren't officially separated, poor woman..."

"Oh, we forgot to mention his Kaluga guy, Gera or Gerasim or something. Sounds like a Turgenev character, doesn't he? Gerasim and Mumu."

"Gera is Ivan Ilyich's distant relative, but they were very close..."

"I know. Ilyich brought him in from Kaluga. More like a second cousin twice removed Ilyich was very kind but he didn't have a lot of family... Gera was working here for a while... How many years ago was that? A few? Angela, you must know. You were the closest to Ivan Ilyich."

"Not that close. Right away, after we completed college. Three, maybe four years ago... All that time Gera was under Ivan Ilyich's wing... Gera *is attractive enough, tall, but timid and oh so boring... I just helped Gerasim when he started working here... Ivan Ilyich asked me to sit near him..."*

"Anyway, Gerasim was his caregiver but he cannot replace Praskovia now."

"Such a strange name – Praskovia. Remember The Death of Ivan Ilyich*? Reality is beginning to imitate art! Don't laugh! Somehow, it all seems so strange and so familiar: Ivan Ilyich and Praskovia Fedorovna – Tolstoy's couple.*

"How did Turgenev get into the conversation?"

"Gerasim came from Turgenev's Mumu*. Not all the names coincide."*

"I'm not much of a reader. Maybe you've got something to say, you're our resident intellectual, Eugenia? You read Tolstoy?"

"Before I say anything, please, another cigarette...Yes, I've read The Death of Ivan Ilyich*. I'm not sure I remember the names of all the characters. It was a long time ago. And shut up about me being an intellectual! It's bad enough you think of me that way."*

"Okay, okay... Have another cigarette. Relax and tell us what you remember..."

"Well, as your resident authority, I can confirm the coincidence – Tolstoy's Ivan Ilyich had a wife named Praskovia, and she even had the patronymic Fedorovna."

"Really! That's crazy!"

"Stranger coincidences have happened. Now, wait for it – Tolstoy's Ivan Ilyich, as I recall, had a serf-servant, a guy named Gerasim! It should be impossible, but it is true. Tolstoy's Ivan Ilyich loved his servant, Gerasim, more than anyone in the world, particularly when he was ill and dying."

"Oh, my God! That's bizarre. That's impossible!"

"It's an important book. A masterpiece of literary architecture. Girls, my friend, Boris, the one from the library faculty, he told me that some serious

critics have suggested that the two Tolstoyan men – Gerasim and Ivan Ilyich – had some sort of Freudian thing going on."

"The Tolstoy who created great women like Anna Karenina, he had a powerful wife, Sofia Andreevna…"

"Tolstoy loved the great actress, Sarah Bernhardt, who played Hamlet…"

"Where did you read that?"

"I remember in Tolstoy's story, Praskovia Fedorovna talks about this French actress, coming from her performance…"

"Eugenia, you really are some expert!"

"I have an idea! I will be back soon. The library's close by!"

"There's no time, Angela."

"I didn't expect this when we started talking about a funeral… I am already poisoned by sitting here smoking for twenty minutes. Let me say this: we know nothing of our Ivan Ilyich's private life with his Praskovia. Once, I watched their faces through a glass wall as they had a vicious fight. They were still living together at the time."

"Oh, shut up. We don't know anything about them! Their private lives are not ours to discuss. Listen, I can't say this out loud…"

"What's the gossip?"

"I just saw our departed, neurotic genius, Vladimir Pavlovich, waiting outside the door of 'King' Mikhail Semenovich. He probably smelled us in here burning away our work hours. Pavlovich, Pavlovich!"

"Eugenia – is there a Vladimir Pavlovich in Tolstoy's novella?"

"No."

"Are you sure? Too bad."

"Tolstoy must have missed him. He's everywhere. So, Vladimir Pavlovich is not a Tolstoyan character. He is not trapped in someone else's story and he's got to create his own destiny, serve his own plot. Like us. He is the master of his own fate."

"Vladimir Pavlovich…should I really envy whoever's going to replace Ivan Ilyich in this reality? I mean, will he inherit that very nice leather office chair. I once made a telephone call from Ilyich's office while sitting in that fantastic chair… It was an amazing experience for my poor little bum, so used to our hard chairs."

"That's no way to talk on the day of Ivan Ilyich's funeral. You should be ashamed of yourself. He's not even stiff and already you've got your ass in his chair. Glafira, you can be so thoughtless. Passionate Lubov will get the leather chair. She hates us women, hates all our bantering."

"Calm down, girls. Natasha is coming down the corridor. She'll hear us and…"

"Natasha. Come on in for a smoke."

"Thanks, but no thanks. I'm busy. Mikhail Semenovich, along with Lubov Arkadievna, wants to invite all of you to join us in planning a memorial for our late Ivan Ilyich."

"Time to butt out."

"Please, girls, come along. Eugenia, don't light up another. It's time for the meeting. I'm on orders."

"Natasha worries so much about orders. Girls, butt out and march on…"

"I am not finished. I'll catch up with you. Have a second cigarette. Natasha… I'll finish, then I'll go."

"Eugenia, you are incorrigible…we love you nonetheless."

"Are you back, Angela? Brought the book?"

"Are you alone, Eugenia? I fetched the book and found a passage where Praskovia Fedorovna talks about Sarah Bernhardt."

"Angela! We've got to run!"

A second, listen: *"Praskovia is in full evening dress, and Ivan remembers that she and the children...*

"Okay! I remember...!"

"Just this! Please, listen to: "...and the children are going to the theatre to see Sarah Bernhardt..."

"We missed you on our break. Natasha rounded up the others. I'm finishing my smoke."

"Strange!"

"Angela, give me your hand and keep running! I know. Sarah Bernhardt was visiting the town and they have a box, which Ivan Ilyich had insisted on their taking... Nothing special."

"Turn into this corridor! It's closer!"

"We need to catch up and offer our respects to the memory of Ivan Ilyich. He was a good man, that Ivan Ilyich...

IX

Interlude

The words of a young woman:

I am your Love and I am here because you have the joy in your heart that is the tower of Konkovo-Derevlevo that you scaled in darkness and the joy that lies in the power of becoming a Russian troubadour whose pipe will play the haunting music of Russian architecture as it dances, yes, with the beasts of the Konkovo forest and yes, dances with me to the heights of beauty and imagination and flies with me through the vertigo of success to the heavens of invention and fame and the vanity that surges in me as I climb from floor to floor through troubled dreams among drafts and sketches and reams of tracing papers amid the clouds of those free conceptualizations that constitute Love and yes, Love raised heartbeat by heartbeat until we see how Love sustains as you feed this brainchild of your genius to the cold whims of time and fate while holding me your love in your heart clothed and fed by everything you have filled with the love found in concrete structures grey and motionless as winter as they conjure and walk the delicate fulcrum points of ideas filled with the happiness that is located in the strength of a steady beam or a horizontal plane that by its very natures declares "I am made of love!" Vladimir Pavlovich! Fly to your next twelve storeys and sing of each as if it has its own life on another step toward a glory alive and reborn with each inch reaching always reaching higher and seeking more love in every aspect of its making! Set aside insult and hatred and envy and pride by spiraling higher and higher in your tower through a darkness lit by red stars shining on the Kremlin's towers...

"The Kremlin," you said? And smiled. "*That's so patriotic.*"

X

Nightfall when Vladimir Pavlovich came home. No food, no appetite. He'd had a late lunch. Opening the fridge, he took several swallows of a cold beer and walked into the empty bedroom… Thank God his wife had gone to see her sister in Kazan. Vladimir Pavlovich. was glad to be alone. He fell onto the soft mattress of the daybed, still wearing his new tweed jacket and new silk tie. He looked at the corner of the ceiling where the walls met, and felt a sense of mad connections…the top, or inner ceiling, of his tower, his obsession, the Konkovo-Derevlevo… Studio 20's swan song… Vladimir Pavlovich couldn't close his eyes. He hated these three intersecting planes – two converging walls and this triangular piece of ceiling held together by a band of angles.

He turned onto his left side…

"Maybe Valocordin? A bit of barbiturate…"

He swallowed ten drops in water and returned to bed…

"Valocordin is good on extreme occasions. Visions of the Youth Palace! Ivan Ilyich, stubborn old adversary – you died. Can't take your victories with you? Please go away! Give me a chance to make a small change at the building site… This is mine, not yours. My Konkovo is still in progress! Go away, let me sleep, stop haunting me with your ideas…accusations implied…"

Vladimir Pavlovich was quiet. Breathing unbroken. Already asleep? Yes, or so he thought. Anna Karenina watches the same ceiling corner in her bedroom… Anna hated her vision just as much as Vladimir Pavlovich hates his. But then, sharply in focus in her mind, Vronsky's gloves! He left them in her lobby, hurrying to his fiancée…

Gloves? It was a cold November... Vladimir Pavlovich is still a student...
his memory friend, Boris, cries out:

"Vladimir! Go to the Serpukhovsky Store! The leather gloves there are
beautiful and warm. They're made in Romania. You hate your knitted mittens
so much..."

"Thanks, Boris!" (The next day he left his new gloves in a phone booth.)
Modulating chords:
Bong! Boom! Bong!

Three? Midnight? A slant. Maybe early morning. This carousel with
Semenovich...the Zholtovsky portrait...a new smoking room, and what
more...what more? Yes. The death of Ivan Ilyich...why is the light still on?
Why didn't I turn it off? So hard to stand...damned light. It will help my
eyes to adjust in case Ivan Ilyich comes to rattle his chains. No. He's not a
ghost who comes through the wall or through the ceiling or through that
corner pretending to be the top of Konkovo-Derevlevo Tower... Ivan Ilyich
is dead. This is the death of Ivan Ilyich. Do I not remember the novella by
Tolstoy? So many things echo each other. Life echoing art and art echoing
life:

Boom! Bong! Boom!

The Kremlin bells sound through the Moscow sky and no one can dream.
Ivan Ilyich is in the morgue... Ivan Ilyich is cold and stiff...is it really him...
who is the real Ivan Ilyich... Tolstoy's? I hear his footsteps! Modulating, ringing
chords! Solid, solemn, grave, basso:

Bong! Bong! Bong!

The tolling tower! The sound of the Kremlin Saviour! The Derevlevo small
tower? A great idea – for Konkovo-Derevlevo, a tolling clock tower! It would
have sounded:

Boom! Boom! Boom!

"I know it is three a.m. I know I am home and not in Red Square... By losing my mind I may find myself. I am me, therein the mystery."

Again, clear, distinct steps...the footsteps of Ivan Ilyich. He's already at the bedroom door.

Vladimir Pavlovich is not afraid... He thinks he sees Ivan Ilyich...moves closer to the bedroom chair...guest or ghost? There is no smirk on the old dead face... Ivan Ilyich stares at Vladimir Pavlovich, he has cold, empty eyes. He stands up and steps back... The door shuts. The echo of the elevator's descent:

Boom! Boom! Boom!

Three o'clock was one or two hours ago. Now it may be five... Through the bedroom's crepuscular hours, Vladimir Pavlovich keeps track of the three bells of the wall clock:

Dizzy, unstable, and shaking, Vladimir Pavlovich goes to the window. The bright, icy moon cuts the black sky. Sharp shadows angle into sharp shadows in the backyard. Where had Vladimir Pavlovich seen such shadows? German Expressionism. Dr. Caligari... Caligari... At the Institute of Cinematography when he was still a student... But now Ivan Ilyich sits on a bench in a children's playground, Vladimir Pavlovich's residential building... Stubborn old man! Why didn't he keep to the morgue?

"I need sleep, I am a watchman at the window. I ask you politely, please go away, stay away, stay my dear dead friend..."

But Vladimir Pavlovich hears:

"Pavlovich, leave me alone! Get a new life..."

A voice lying low. As if spoken through wet paper.

"A bracelet of bright hair about the bone, it burns."

Who said this? A moonlit backyard full of trash containers, that's where Ivan Ilyich is resting. Barking, growling. Agile animals, shattering the stillness *as they hunt for food. Behind the dilapidated fence, the centre of the nearest road is striped. Lusterless streetlamps… Ivan Ilyich sits in the backyard. Is he dead? Ivan Ilyich: when and why did you die? No. Maybe Ivan Ilyich dreamed he was a dead man…a dream in his head. Maybe in mine, too.*

The moon slides behind the clouds. Vladimir Pavlovich sees the Youth Palace! Ivan Ilyich is motionless as the shadow of a building. He sighs dead breath. He is fluttering his hands like the conductor of a symphonic death chord:

Boom! Boom! Boom!

"Pavlovich! Sleep! You are my enemy, my friend."

For many minutes there is silence…but again, the dead man's voice:

"Is it not enough for you to triumph as the creator of Konkovo-Derevlevo? I made all that possible. Greedy demon! Sleep! You won the competition for the tower because I am dead, also – thanks to your faith in that American, Mies van der Rohe, his hanging walls. Many of the project judges haven't adapted to him yet…they don't like him…but they will… Your love of our great Russian, Zholtovsky, is the key to how you lie! You claim to love Zholtovsky! You are a liar! You resurrected the corpse of Stalinist Gothic, five-storey, contemporary industrial huts! Shameful. God damn the Thaw! Sleep.

Shivering, his body hot, sweaty. A fever lacking temperature. Vladimir Pavlovich lifts heavy eyelids. Where is he? Home. Thank God, in his bedroom. On his bed. The burning light is too bright. He screws up his eyes. What happened? What time is it? Is it still night? Why didn't he take off his shoes? Tingling ankles, a prickling in his feet…pain in all his joints and muscles…it is too hard to crawl on the floor. Shaking, Vladimir Pavlovich approaches the window. Night is still behind it. He pushes the window open partway. The air is chilly. The night smells of June and penetrates his lungs. Smells brush against his sleeping face. His brain doesn't realize he has had a nightmare. He pinches his cheek. Painful. He looks down from his open window. Night is ready to meet the day, a slight rosy line in the low clouds. The moon is still high, slowly slipping, slipping away…

Vladimir Pavlovich went to the funeral. Natasha had called him. It was around nine. After such a bad night, he needed to get going. He'd had enough of bed terror!

Should he continue to seek redemption through real life? Could there be good terror? He's opening the door to the sorrowful ritual. It is underway. He can see the body of Ivan Ilyich… Vladimir Pavlovich… His eyes blind after the nightmare… He realizes he cannot recognize his colleagues gathered in the room. He is sure all members of Studio 20 are there. He needs to see the corpse up close…to see how death has transformed the man…to grapple with how life is changed to death. What does the sheen on the skin – the alabaster sheen – mean? Is the sheen light?

Vladimir Pavlovich stands by the corpse, focused on the unmoving face, on the dead architect's functionless body. Sucking for air, close to collapse. Again, he is haunted by a Youth Palace mistake in design, a flawed structure, an inept project... His almost friend is steady as stone. Is the body a spectre out of German Expressionism, not merely a man reducing himself to dust but a mirage? Maybe he has simply closed his eyes, and the world has gone out like a light, not Ivan Ilyich. Vladimir Pavlovich bends to bring his forehead close to the corpse, he kisses the forehead, shaking with loathing, then steps back a little to gaze on the still face of the dead. Sorry, he thinks to himself as he addresses Leo Tolstoy who presides over such matters of love and death. Help me to understand this sad vision:

The dead man lay, as dead men always lie, in a specially heavy way, his rigid limbs sunk in the soft cushions of the coffin, with the head forever bowed on the pillow. His yellow waxen brow with bald patches over his sunken temples was thrust up in the way peculiar to the dead, the protruding nose seeming to press on the upper lip. He was much changed and grown even thinner since...but, as is always the case with the dead, his face was handsomer and, above all, more dignified than when he was alive. The expression on the face said that what was necessary had been accomplished, and accomplished rightly.

Besides this there was in that expression a reproach and a warning to the living. This warning seemed out of place, or at least, not applicable to him. He felt a certain discomfort and so he hurriedly crossed himself once more and turned and went out of the front door – too hurriedly and too regardless of propriety, as he himself was aware.

Caught in a daylight nightmare after a sleep, Vladimir Pavlovich could not find rest, nor any comfort in death, but only wandered through a pale shadowed conversation with the dead, with speechless jesters, with mourners among the living who stood or shuffled, captivated for the moment by the dead, uttering short eulogies, an odd tirade, tears amidst a shallows of sighs, silence, incomprehension. The mourners overwhelmed him…and then they asked Vladimir Pavlovich to speak. They touched his hands, shook his hand, squeezed him…someone stroked his hair, kissed him…women, men, even children with their attending parents…mostly unknown faces… Vladimir Pavlovich recognized a woman running through the crowd… Praskovia Fedorovna? Yes. In black, looking younger than when he'd last seen her working in Studio 20…all were in some way connected to Studio 20 and the creative life of Ivan Ilyich…involved in this incomprehensible ritual…attending to a death.

Vladimir Pavlovich had to get away, get away and get out of his imagination! Having been so close to the motionless thing in the coffin…death had touched him, made him feel that a small part of himself was dying…is dying, slowly…

Suddenly he is held by familiar hands…his wife? He hardly recognizes her…she looks so strange…When did she come back to Moscow? Did something happen to her sister, making her come so quickly from Kazan? Who's the woman talking so seriously to his wife? Lubov Arkadievna. She, too, is dressed in black. She whispers something into his wife's ear, nodding with an apologetic smile…such a strange smile…lingering in Vladimir Pavlovich's mind, that strange, apologetic smile…

XII

Reality, fantasy? Who can tell? Who needs to tell? A break in the sequence of running days... We come to the moment when we must examine the brief writing career of Vladimir Pavlovich. Maybe his Moscow typewriter has broken. Maybe he has left the Research Project Institute and the Optima typewriter behind. Why is this portion of the narrative not in italics?

We all know time flies...that's why it's a cliché...it contains an eternal nub of conventional wisdom... A day, two, three, maybe more. A month? A year? A world of words and pages, it collapses faster than the memories it attempts to animate. It quickens like the living while becoming motionless like the dead. A stasis at the heart of the cyclone. The typed sheets are on the table...they are ready to come to the end of this story...the final pages describing how Vladimir Pavlovich visited the funeral of Ivan Ilyich, his late, lamented, almost friend, who was both honoured and disdained among the living.

But where is Vladimir Pavlovich? Some people who were his colleagues in Studio 20 or were mere acquaintances, say that he is okay. What do they know? When even he doesn't know. Is he a writer? That remains to be seen. Maybe he is back at Studio 20, dreaming of modern industrial cathedrals, all racing the wind into the sky, newer, higher, spurred on by the wax wings of his imagination. Maybe, he is still standing, dumbstruck at the funeral for Ivan Ilyich, fixated on the mystery of death, and wordless in the face of a body about to become dust. Maybe all suggestions are idle speculation, rumours that run rampant among those who barely know what's what with whom and where?

Someone says Vladimir Pavlovich is a writer. Maybe not. Maybe he is sitting in the comfortable leather chair that once belonged to Ivan Ilyich.

Framed, and next to the portrait of Zholtovsky, is a portrait of the late, lamented Ivan Ilyich. Vladimir Pavlovich, smiles at those who come into his office. He is careful when it comes to smiles…he hoards them, measures them out, maintains a professional, creative distance.

"Ah, Lubov Arkadievna, please come in! For you I am free. The result of our recent competition with Studio 10 has just come to me. Congratulations! Yes, the normal bonus. Is the Subaru okay? You can choose something different, perhaps a cottage for your relatives from another city, for instance?"

"How about you, dear Vladimir Pavlovich?"

"Me? This doesn't matter… I prefer an austere Volvo, stealing down the Russian forest roads…if I had my choice in the matter…"

"You love to live modestly, Vladimir Pavlovich."

"Closer to nature. Always, I'm studying nature…"

He let his smile linger in the air.

XIII

A bright, almost blinding light. The fresh, green, splendid foliage of trees abounds. Probably, it is June. A June from some years ago... The silky grass touches the sandaled feet of two men. They are strolling, enjoying this divine landscape. One holds a book that has a leather cover. The second waves the twig from an exotic tree. They discuss the layout of the Acropolis, they try to count up all the ancient Greek temples, including those demolished or destroyed by time or wars. They recall and reconstruct, in words, the shape, structure, colour and details of the ruined promontory. They are Ivan Ilyich and Ivan Vladislavovich, the latter known as the architect Zholtovsky...

They stop, look around. Zholtovsky is slightly worried:

ZHOLTOVSKY:
Who or what is following us? Like a dense cloud, a dark shade, close in pursuit, so persistent...

IVAN ILYICH:
Behind? Above? Who is it? Many among the living are saying goodbye to their lives...but they are not ready to join us. Maybe, my friend, my colleague, and master architect, a good man is sickly but ambitious. He is still naked on his ascent into our holy land... In my past life, I went through a period of creative harmony and then a cleft in time full of dissonance...as a result, my farewell bordered on the tragic...and now, that man who was there to say goodbye to me wants to come to us, I

recall the sonorous toll of the Kremlin Saviour Tower bell – solemn, grave:

Clang! Clang! Clang!

ZHOLTOVSKY:
He should be in no hurry, whoever he is. He'll get here all in good time.

IVAN ILYICH:
Is Vladimir Pavlovich an admirer of yours, Ivan Vladislavovich? Your Stalinist Renaissance revival inspired him. He went to Italy, retraced your itinerary – wanted to know what you had known, learn what you had learned. He saw Palladio's work in Venice and Vincenza. He was passionate about your style. It became the whole engine of his being.

ZHOLTOVSKY:
Intriguing...someone remembers me...do you remember my speech to the Moscow Architects? I forget. Sometime in the middle Fifties. You were there. And if he hears us now, I can repeat it all, verbatim:

Architecture is called upon to create structures for enjoying life, not just for people who are living now, but for future generations also.

IVAN ILYICH:
Bravo!

ZHOLTOVSKY:
The Renaissance is alive now. In Italy, certainly...but especially in our great Russia! It lives in my structures, in the Soviet buildings of the Fifties. Now, there's this pure art. They called it Stalinist Gothic!

IVAN ILYICH:
Pure!

ZHOLTOVSKY:
Depends on your angle of vision. It's serious. It was 1925. I went to Italy to
see Palladio's work in Venice! Those were the days. We thought there were
endless possibilities, we were going to reinvent the great ages in our works
and in our time. Hustling through those narrow little lanes, I leapt into a
gondola. I cried: "Young gondolier, do you know – Venice is built on Siber-
ian larch, it's a wood as hard as iron? There were 400,000 ironwood logs
from outside the Angara River driven into that salt marsh at the head of
the Adriatic. They were brought to Venice starting in the Fifth century...
Venice was built on such a foundation...roofed in the soil of Mother
Russia."

IVAN ILYICH:
Ah, yes, but who hauled that unique wood to Venice? Nobody knows. We
lose so much as we lose time.

ZHOLTOVSKY:
Gondolier, you should learn Russian and sing in Russian, sing your song
in the tongue of your city's roots. Not understanding what I'd said, he sang:

Sing, sing – there's now nowhere to go...
Venezia mine,
You made me fall in love...

IVAN ILYICH:

Bravo! I wonder whether St. Peter loves it, too...and whether he likes the story of it being Russian wood that keeps this city afloat on pastel waters of its own reflection?

ZHOLTOVSKY:

Singing an Italian song is giving voice to great art! And architecture is music, too. I listened to the Italian songs of the Renaissance and I wanted my buildings, my designs, my works, to be a hymn to life, not only for people to behold, but to live in, to work in! Imagine being embraced by music as beautiful as the light of stars.

IVAN ILYICH:

You were so happy before we came to this world! Ironically, that brute, Stalin, saved you and your vision. I led a slightly different life, but I was happy, too...

ZHOLTOVSKY:

I can't count how many times the secret police questioned me. It was a time when so many went silent. My attitude was relief, maybe even gratitude, because in that terrible silence I was able to speak through my works. It was my special time. My happiness was built on seeing and loving the great Palladio. On my knees and in tears, I prayed in Palladio's San Giorgio Maggiore in Venice. And I brought the bell tower behind it to Moscow! My vision honoured – my dream – honoured by Smolensky House, my tower...

IVAN ILYICH:

Our iconic monument...

ZHOLTOVSKY:

Remember Gogol? *"Architecture is a chronicle of the world: it speaks when songs and legends are silent."*

IVAN ILYICH:

The sound of Gogol's *Dead Souls* in Italy. But your voice – your reverence for Andrea Palladio, it humbles me. I spoke to the Moscow Arch-Council on behalf of Vladimir Pavlovich's tower on the Konkovo!

Vladimir Pavlovich's voice (as if uttered in a muted thought): I can hear you talking in my thoughts. Past friends, future friends in eternity!

IVAN ILYICH:

Are you anywhere close by? You're always in a hurry. Don't be in such a hurry to join up with us. We're eternal, time means nothing to us. While it means everything to you, and you'd better make good use of it. Take a deep breath, go out for a stroll the grass. Breathe! Breathe! In heaven, the air is thin...later...we can discuss your Youth Palace.

ZHOLTOVSKY:

Was that Vladimir Pavlovich?

IVAN ILYICH:

He's on the waiting list. Saint Peter is so busy. Madcap times, I guess. So many candidates waiting to be called. Him, I'm not so sure about. Maybe he'll join us. Ivan Vladislavovich, let's go up Cypress Alley and see who the newcomers are.

SAINT PETER:

Please, Ivan Vladislavovich, take it easy, you've been here longer than you think. Take a seat under these holy trees. Kick back in the shade.

ZHOLTOVSKY:

Saint Peter! You're still making Christ look really good...

SAINT PETER:

Who's that with you? My goodness, Ivan Ilyich, so soon. Zholtovsky – times are going to be good for our architectural community. I wish you both a pleasant afterlife!

IVAN ILYICH:

Leo Tolstoy was right: How good and how simple... And my pain? What has become of it? Where is your pain? And death? Where is it? ...Death is finished. It is no more...

SAINT PETER:

Next! Oh, there you are, Vladimir Pavlovich. While you're waiting, try to do something about envy and ambition. When your time comes, I'll take you down our Holy Cypress Alley, but not yet. Keep to your own body and your own head.

VLADIMIR PAVLOVICH:

But I've been waiting and waiting and I'm afraid I'll lose touch with my friends...

SAINT PETER:

Always anxious. Always brimming with perplexing thoughts, your worrisome energy. I don't recall you calling Ivan Ilyich your friend. Adversary, or...almost a friend is more like it. Work on that. More meditation wouldn't hurt. In the meantime, don't worry. You'll get here sooner than you think, the Lord willing. Don't block the way. Next!

FINAL CHAPTER: VERSION ONE

The morning rush-hour Moscow Metro is crowded...so crowded...crazy Moscow! How many millions? Every year, the population explodes. Vladimir Pavlovich catches sight of someone familiar, a face among faces! That's him, his former colleague, a young architect. Can't remember his last name. Near enough. A sudden recollection: Peter of the notorious Studio 20. Yes, that's him!

"Nice to see you, Peter!"

"Vladimir Pavlovich. Glad to see you, too!"

"Haven't seen you for a while. I've been planning to drop by to visit my former workshop. What's that? Can't hear you. So much noise!"

"Come see us, Vladimir Pavlovich, come see Ivan Ilyich!"

"What happened to him?"

"He just turned sixty! No invitation? You should've got it. I saw your name on the list...you're invited. My stop! See you soon..."

The young man, thrust onto the platform by the crowd, disappears. Vladimir Pavlovich turns to the dark window. He stares at his image in the glass, all his thoughts and fantasies in a pre-revolutionary Tolstoyan dream world crushed by reality.

I am sorry, Ivan Ilyich, for putting you through the perils of my imagination. Long life to you, Ivan Ilyich! Sixty is a good age for a creative working architect. May we live in the real world of Soviet culture!

The morning rush-hour Moscow Metro is crowded. Standing on the platform for some twenty minutes, Vladimir Pavlovich is late for his job. Three trains go by and he cannot get on. Crowded! Crazy Moscow! How many millions in Moscow? Every year the number grows... Okay, this train...the door opens. Vladimir Pavlovich is shoved by a lady carrying two huge bags. Trying to cross the threshold, he feels a hand on his arm. Vladimir Pavlovich is in the car, he's sitting between strangers. Who touched him?

"Peter, hello! We meet again, so soon. It was just a couple of days ago. Is Ivan Ilyich ready for his sixtieth birthday party?"

"Ivan Ilyich is dead. The funeral will be tomorrow."

"Impossible. I was going to go to his party."

Vladimir Pavlovich could not say, "I knew this would happen."

He could not say, "This is the end I have already written for my story."

Vladimir Pavlovich could not say, "It is my future, meeting like this and you telling me of the death of Ivan Ilyich, telling me that he's gone to join Zholtovsky in the school of architects who dream of structures without substance and sites without place."

Vladimir Pavlovich could not say, "That we should meet like this, it's my future."

Instead he said: "Yes, this is really sad."

Vladimir Pavlovich thought: "Ivan Ilyich died just as I finished typing on that old Optima. Could there be another way to end this story?"

No words.

Both – Vladimir Pavlovich with two unfinished buildings behind him and the young architect, Peter (is he Tolstoy's Peter Ivanovich, is he still young?), two Russian architects of the Seventies who worked for Studio 20

– one morning both sat facing the carriage window on a crowded Moscow Metro train. Both shared a silence they could not fill with words, sitting together for a couple of stops as the train shook beneath the foundations of the great buildings of Moscow. That is all. There is no more to tell, except to say Ivan Ilyich was remembered at Studio 20 by the girls in the smoking room and the clerks sorting papers among endless files. And Gerasim, Ivan Ilyich's adopted nephew, sat by a window on a June morning, his day off, and he stared with reverence at the pages of a book bequeathed to him by his erstwhile uncle who had meditated upon the fabled towers of Italy.

An Atomic Cake

There are children playing in the streets who could solve some of my top problems in physics, because they have modes of sensory perception that I lost long ago.

—ROBERT OPPENHEIMER

ONE
A LONG PROLOGUE

How to begin, what to call this work?
Tap, tap…
Margarita Cocktail – tap
Rita-Margarita – dancing
(A chiming rhyme)
Also, "Rio Rita"

Which was an old-time dance tune
Danced by my parents under the moon of the Forties,
The Montevideo Tango, 78s spinning
(You needed new steel needles
And more new needles).
But right now (a highly suspect ploy), I'm
Working on a period of my life,
At a time
When "cocktail" had
Entered the Moscow idiom of alcoholic joy.
    1963. Back in the city –
    A place long on police, short on pity.
    After three years of architectural
Work for the Soviet Republic of Ukraine,
I was hanging out with
Free-thinking students who were
Bent on unbending the truth
In a notorious vodka house
On Gorky Street, close by the Kremlin,

A getaway haunt for "parasitical" youth –
Political gremlins of the future –
While the Great Fellini and his wife, Masina, stood on stage at
The Kremlin Palace[1], in the shadow of several steeples,
All smiles, on behalf of and at the behest
Of the Moscow International Film
Festival, Best Film, *8½*,
So said the International jury,
Proxy for our Soviet Ministry
Of Culture, whose First Minister, Furtseva,
Engaging in "space chats,"
Had introduced to the Festival guests
Yuri Gagarin as he stepped,
Bubble-hat under his arm, onto the "flat" earth.
We had also heard of André Breton's *Nadja*,
Henry Moore's sculpture
And on the heels of *La Strada*
Came *Samizdat*[2]:
A scurrilous, underground publishing house,
Limited to only 125 members, distributing 140 tissue-
Thin copies of each issue.
Meanwhile, The Moscow Art Theatre[3]
Is about to perform Mikhail
Bulgakov's version of Gogol's
Dead Souls. Bulgakov!
Always lurking, year after year, in the Moscow shadows,
In lockstep
With his giant Cat, Behemoth[4].

Such was life.

After a long political cold front, that is, the Stalinist winter,

An ordered chaos had emerged

Out of Premier Nikita Sergeyevich Khrushchev's Thaw.

Novi mir[5] the *nouvelle vague* Fellini, Yevtushenko...

Life could be a dream.

Life could be a film. Noir.

Eyes wide open!

Two words: Margarita Cocktail.

At that time, there was

No USSR wine worth drinking.

Mr. Glen Fiddich of Dufftown, and Mr. Jack Daniels of Kentucky

Were on the shelf. For special money called

Certificates, good drink could

Be had, brought home from Business abroad.

Vodka, the Russian Man's close companion

Was always there grinning, to ward off death,

But cocktails...cocktails became one with joy!

In Moscow, heart beating beneath the

Snaggle-toothed red-brick Kremlin walls, I went

For a stroll, along Sadovaya Ring Road[6]

Past brutalist skyscrapers cropping up

On Moscow's Seven Holy Hills

(Topographical imitation of Jerusalem).

EUREKA! – A proposition

Drinks all 'round.
Cocktails for two. And more.
A Margarita Cocktail was
Named in honour of the actress Rita Hayworth!
Hollywood diva,
Very popular after 1946 – after the Atomic Test at Bikini Atoll.
Rita Hayworth's image – *GILDA* – had been glued
To one of the Bombs! American Military Men drank
Margarita Cocktails to celebrate Gilda's ascension into heaven!

All of a sudden I'd found a friend –

ARTHUR

A young member of the Moscow Math Faculty,
First to utter in my presence the magic word

COMPUTER

He asked:

> *"Vladimir, your opinion, the best movie in the world, is it not*
> Potemkin?"[7]

> "Potemkin? *No*," I said. *"The best film is,*
> Citizen Kane!"

As one of the Thaw generation, Arthur was
Partial to *Potemkin,* and
To Italian New Realism, *cinema verité,*
Sartre's Existentialism, the "absurd" (Muscovite normalcy) –
What did I know? – Arthur's cry:
    "*Potemkin!*
    Potemkin!"
"*No! The best movie,*" I said, "*is*
Citizen Kane. *Orson Welles. Believe me!*"

And that was that, our Thaw talk for the day.

A visit to Arthur's home.
1946: In the dark. "*Shh…something's afoot."*   MEOW.
His mother showed me a
Photo album brought by Arthur's
Father from Atoll Bikini in the
Pacific – where he'd been the Soviet observer
At the American TESTING of the ATOMIC BOMB!

The early Sixties. As I've said, I'd come to Moscow
From exile in Ukraine, to work as a young architectural innovator,
To deconstruct the conventional
Sombre construction of all too glum Moscow.
Something a little lunatic was also loose in the air.
Amidst it all, Arthur, with
His futurological fantasies. A young Russian Jules Verne.
Proclaiming:

"All the Johannes Guttenberg
Papers will be put to the fire!

"Hail to a Great Upheaval!
The new Leviathon, the

COMPUTER!"

Back then
At my study table
I sat reading Chekhov's Anya Monologue!
The city was on *dimmer*.
Muscovites asleep.

CATWALK

Anything can happen in the nighttime –

A giant cat is crawling across a flat roof –
It descends. Down a drain pipe.

Bulgakov's Behemoth is out on night
Patrol. Men have their ears to the wall.
The Cat purrs into the phone.
He has the voice of a kitten.
He opens his green eyes –
And says:

> *"Arthur, you shall end up in New York.*
> *Vladimir, get to work!"*

TWO
VLADIMIR GETS TO KNOW ARTHUR

Snippets of stories, it's the best I can do.

> *All the Johannes Guttenberg Papers*
> *Will be put to the fire.*
> *Long live the COMPUTER.*

Arthur! Ten years my junior. Who am I? I am who I am –
My canonical, iconic, inner life
Attuned to the Doric, Toscana, Jonick, Corinthian columns –

Arthur, believing he is so ahead of me, ahead of his place, up-to-date
with his time…

> THE SEAGRAM BUILDING –
> SKYSCRAPER LOCATED AT 375 PARK AVENUE
> BETWEEN 52ND AND 53RD STREETS
> MANHATTAN, NEW YORK CITY.
> MIES VAN DER ROHE.
> INTERNATIONAL STYLE!

ARTHUR the INVINCIBLE:

> *"You, Vladimir, you are not*
> *Electro-programmable! Typographical*
> *Chaos is about to come. It is already here.*
> *'A period is like a bullet,' said Babel.*[8]

There's a time coming of indiscriminate period fire.
Scatter-shot typography all over the page. Sign of the times.

Sixties Moscow.
Winter.
Breathing in ice on the air.

> *"Vladimir! Remember where you ate when*
> *You were a student?"*

Petrovka![9]
Near my institute –
Monthly scholarship, twenty-two roubles –
Four roubles spent on soup – *solyanka!*
Fresh sturgeon!
Glint of black olives, glint of fish scales, direct from the fire.

> *"What's the problem?"*

> *"I've got an extra ticket to Tchaikovsky Hall."*

> *"Okay, I work quite close by, Mayakovsky Square. But for what?"*

> *"French Ballet."*

> *"Sorry! I'm no balletomane,"*

> *"But the music – Debussy, Ravel! Come on, it's from Paris."*

We were only recently allowed to listen to this music.

Next evening:

People of presence, influence.
Elegance had long since become a lost echo
Of itself. As yet, no recruits to the zoot suit.
Double-breasted, big lapels.
A loud female voice:

>   *"Vladimir!"*

There are Vladimirs all over Moscow!
Vlad, Vlad, Vlad, you can go crazy.
I can go crazy.

A STOLID WOMAN:

>   *"Hello Vladimir! Arthur pointed you out. I am his mother.*
>   *Galina Ivanovna. It's so cold! Please, inside!"*

He'd come with his mother!
Orchestra at eye level, so close to the stage.
How much did such tickets cost?
The lights dim to darkness,
A tense stillness. Arthur's husky breathing.
Bright lights!
A forest unnaturally aglow. A wild animal. A Faun.
A French dancer is *en pointe* to

Debussy. A Faun wearing Dutch cow spots.

This is the Thaw. A Faun dressed up like a cow.

Arthur and his mother.

Applause, applause...

THREE
POETRY AT PAVELETSKY[10]

My phone is connected.
Still, we are all disconnected. One day, we're in Roman, the next in *italics*.
No one calls or visits my home
Located on the Ring Road.

Later –
Passing through this area with a co-student,
I pointed:

> *"Remember Arthur? Our young science guy?*
> *He lives here! In this big building."*

> *"You sure? It's where secret, very private people live.*
> *Didn't you know?"*

My own room, fourteen metres,
Two doors into the corridor, open to neighbours.
I had a phone, so I called:

> *"Arthur, you free? After your lectures?*
> *Come on over tonight?*
> *Take the trolley bus – it's only fifteen minutes.*
> *Some new friends, guys who like poetry."*

> *"Poetry? Forget it!*
> *Though I remember a Pushkin poem."*

"It is enough!"

I had this inexplicable interest in poetry.
I'd been reading novels, psychology, history at
The Lenin Library,
And
Poetry came to me via Alisa!
At the wedding of a friend's friend.
She smoked long cigarettes. A cigarette-holder.
Very red lips! Dancing, I tried to hold
   Her body close.

     "Stop! I am a lesbian. And a poet."

     "A poet?"

In my room, all fourteen metres, a poet!
LITTLE GIRL VOICE:

     "Hey, you guys!
     I got a poem published in our gazette, 'The Worker!'
     Do you know that Apollinaire
     Had a Russian mother? Served in the Tsarist Army!
     Meanwhile,
     For tonight, I will read our great Akhmatova,
     New poems, here on these rice
     Paper sheets from Samizdat,
     Sacred truth, still alive.
     Akhmatova: her soul is so close to mine:

'My husband whipped me with a belt,
Tooled leather, twisted-in-two.
I sat at a window waiting for you
All night, till daybreak. Above the smelter…'

"Vladimir, why don't you read something too?"

"How about some more Akhmatova:

'And Pushkin's exile had begun here,
And Lermontov's expulsion ended here.
Amidst the easeful scent of highland grass.
And only once did I happen to pass.'"

FOUR
FIRST VISIT TO ARTHUR'S PLACE

Christmas? No such thing as Christmas in our
Godless country. THE GREAT HOLIDAY –
Arthur's RESIDENCE,
Dimly lit:

> *"Vladimir? Why are you in Moscow?"*

> *"I'm studying, Galina Ivanovna."*

> *"You have a very Russian Name –*
> *Vladimir!… I didn't want to call my son 'Arthur'!"*

> *"Mama!"*

> *"I just wish to say – ARTHUR was his father's idea.*
> *Mikhail Arkadievich, our famous Soviet physicist,*
> *he was obsessed with English history.*
> *King Arthur! The Round Table! Camelot!"*

> *"Mama!"*

> *"Mikhail Arkadievich wanted to be reborn in Camelot!*
> *A Soviet King among Soviet Knights!"*

> *"Mother."*

"Mikhail Arkadievich went to work at the Round Table of our time, the United Nations!"

FIVE
SERMON ON THE MOUNT

ARTHUR's Sermon:

> *"Cybernetics! Computers!*
> *Machines, there can be no doubt*
> *Will be our economic rebooters.*
> *Don't laugh! Our faculty will out-*
> *Pace what seems fantasy within a month or two! Yes!*
> *You, you ignoramus architect! Mindless!*
> *I got permission to attend a foreign presentation,*
> *An invitation to advances in invention..."*

> *"This is all so unreal!"*

> *"This is a cosmic deal.*
> *Remember Lenin's Library, the brutal walls*
> *The study cells, the huge stacks, the book stalls*
> *There'll soon be banks of elegant screens that will occupy*
> *A much smaller space. Say goodbye*
> *To print, to the millions of books, they'll all be on chips!*
> *So much for tradition, for intellectual whistles and whips,*
> *Humankind may be more frenetic*
> *But we shall also be electric, kinetic."*

> *"I'm dizzy."*

Life went on.
I was at home,
A small supper in the common kitchen.
His call. Out of nowhere.

ARTHUR:

"Vladimir, I have free tickets for 'Zero Zero Seven,'
Goldfinger*! In our Science House. Tonight!*
A late Session! – 11:00 p.m.!"

"What movie?"

"Zero Zero Seven?
You Oughta Be Ashamed of Yourself.
The whole world knows about this movie.
Mama'll be there, too!"

Zero Zero Seven,
Made-up words,
Arthur's Informatics. Computer Logic. Mainframe.
Punch Card. Log In.
Crawling in my head.
Brezhnev's[11] lost at sea in a wooden boat. Leakage.

SIX
AUNT MARFA'S BIRTHDAY

ARTHUR:

> *"My mother – Galina Ivanovna –*
> *Would like to see you. A celebration in our family."*

Coming in from the
Sidewalks on a sunny Moscow spring day –
Puddles, streets of puddles
(Solzhenitsyn: A Man does not drown in an ocean,
He drowns in a puddle).
In the crepuscular light of their rooms
Something of the old menace.
It was hard to find slippers to change my shoes.

GALINA IVANOVNA:

> *"Oh Vladimir! Those slippers belonged*
> *To Arthur's father! Very warm."*

Galina Ivanovna embraced me.

> *"So – dear friend! It's my sister Marfa's Birthday!"*

> *"Vladimir, please come to my room!"*

"Arthur, my son, you are unbearable! Vladimir,
This day is about Mikhail Arkadievich being on Bikini Atoll for the
Testing of the American Atomic Bomb!"

"What?"

"The Atomic Bomb on Bikini Atoll."

Arthur's room.
Nothing about the American bomb amidst
Optimistic wall posters.
Walls of typographical terror.
Like the weather, gone amuck.
More *Bold Face*, small caps,
Typography
All downhill.
Slalom to the left. Slalom to the right.
Arthur loved skiing.
And Paul Anka
Between posters of eternal snows on the slopes!

"My father's words:
'Listen to Paul Anka! Not his music.
But his English articulation.'

"I took my father's advice. Anka was my Canadian English teacher.
He placed his phrases perfectly.

"By the way, have you ever seen GILDA*?*
She was a member of the Atomic Party!"

SEVEN
ATOMIC CAKE

GALINA IVANOVNA beaming:

> *"Vladimir! We're chemists —*
> *Be careful about*
> *Chemical reactions..."*

A round table,
On it, an installation,
A cone. Upside down!
A birthday cake?
Vanilla. Sugar icing.
On top,
A wild marzipan mushroom!
Surrounded by sugar stars.

> *"...this is Marfa's birthday Cake.*
> *The Atomic Cake!"*

My reaction? Stillness.

> *"Comrades!*
> *Mikhail Arkadievich,*
> *Left us his Hyper-Delicious*
> *Authentic recipe for the American Atomic*
> *Bomb Test Cake! Such perspicacity."*

Arthur's knife, straight to the heart!
Bewildered, I raise a glass.
Clink of crystal! GALINA IVANOVNA close by my ear:

> *"Vladimir, I am a mother, but I am also a Soviet chemist!*
> *My job after the war!*
> *To evaluate the whole German Cast Iron Industry!*
> *What a job for a woman?"*

> *"Mama…"*

> *"Shut up. He's an architect — about to erect Marxist superstructures*
> *Over the whole of our Communist Future!"*

> *"Hooray!"*

> *"Yes, hooray, my son. But NOW —*
> *Welcome to all of you!*
> *WE JOIN TOGETHER —*
> *Around Mikhail Arkadievich's heritage book…"*

On the table — the photo album!

ARTHUR:

> *"My father brought this document*
> *Back from his American trip as a Soviet physicist.*
> *Look at the cover!*
> *THE ATOMIC BOMB TEST AT BIKINI ATOLL."*

GALINA IVANOVNA:

> *"The photos might be very useful to you*
> *As an architect. New Mexico! Bikini Atoll! What a landscape –*
> *On this page…"*

ARTHUR:

> *"…these are*
> *Bikini aboriginals.*
> *Look at the streaming rivers.*
> *Symbol of a surge of energy for a new*
> *Technology! And the desert! So contemporary.*
> *An absence of absence."*

Arthur smiled.

GALINA IVANOVNA:

> *"It's like the birth of another dimension! The Bomb was ready!*
> *Then the Launch! It rises up. You can follow it, it becomes a cloud.*
> *Growing, growing, working energy!"*

Page by page! Arthur turned…enraptured.

> *"Already the Bomb's got its own halo!*
> *This, this, the flaming white*
> *Mushroom! Blazing!"*

I was
Astonished, saddened,
Downcast. I even felt criminal.
Hiroshima, Nagasaki, as we sat
At the table licking icing.

GALINA IVANOVNA:

"This Album is our ICON!"

EIGHT
KITSCH OR REFINED POLITICS

New times.
We are alone. Except for Elvis.
Elvis on a 78,
Round and round. "Blue Suede Shoes."
"Heartbreak Hotel."
The photo album on the coffee table.
And the Atomic Cake.

ARTHUR:

> *"This photo is my favorite!*
> *The unexpected angle! Like we are inside this*
> *Hot mass of burning gold! Real art!*
> *This is film equipment my father brought from abroad.*
> *I call it my Pandora's box.*
> *From the*
> *Time of the Test. 1946.*
> *Works perfectly!*
> *I was two! Mickey Mouse*
> *Was my Pal."*

VLADIMIR:

> *"Arthur! All I can think of is Hiroshima, Nagasaki!"*

ARTHUR:

"This is photographic Art!"

VLADIMIR:

"This is Dante's Hell, his Inferno. Arthur, for God's sake, I'm a builder!"

He moved the album.
Something fell to the floor.
A small piece of newsprint,
Two large words – HERALD TRIBUNE.

*"My father cut that out of the newspaper. His attitude to the test
Was closer to yours."*

"This is too much for me."

*"I'd like to tell you – what with you being a Soviet architect – life is
Much more complicated than building good solid houses.
My father, my poor father! He was not a revolutionary thinker!
After the test, all he wanted
Was to dream. Never mind.
Look at this headline:*

"THE OPERATION CROSSROADS CELEBRATORY
EVENT TOOK PLACE ON NOVEMBER 5, 1946
AT THE OFFICERS' CLUB IN WASHINGTON.

"And look at the photo!
Don't look at your watch."

"But it's late."

THE COMMANDER OF THE TASK FORCE,
WILLIAM BLANDY, AND HIS WIFE, MRS. BLANDY,
CUTTING THE ATOMIC CAKE.
THE UNUSUAL PASTRY WAS ORDERED
BY STRICT BUSINESS REQUEST!

"You don't understand, Arthur — I've led a different life than you,
I don't believe in the beauty of bombs."

"All our lives, Vladimir, are
Different. My mirror is my father. With Elvis is singing to me."

NINE
ARTHUR SICK

The same brutal winter weather.

PHONE:

> *"Vladimir, I have a fever."*

Galina Ivanovna opened the door.

> *"Vladimir, please come to the kitchen."*

Broth on the boil, cabbage soup called *shchi*.
Pouring tea.
Holding a special glass strainer.

> *"I worked in Germany after the War. A couple of years.*
> *A crazy job! It was so hard! The German language!*
> *But their people are like our people! Why did they love Hitler?*
> *They love herbs like we do. Herbs enrich life.*
> *As a chemist can I tell you — we're artificially impinging on*
> *Life. Thank God for*
> *Health Control, thank God we've rejected antibiotics in our milk!"*

> *"Antibiotics?"*

> *"They're there to keep it fresh longer. And Vladimir.*
> *Don't eat sugar! As an official Soviet chemist, I tell you! Before the War —*

I worked for the Food Industry! No sugar! Poison!
Starting with its manufacture."

"Galina Ivanovna, during the war I dreamed of sugar...
There's someone in the hall."

"Marfa?"

"The Doctor's here, he wants hot water."

"I am boiling a big teapot full as we speak. Mind you, don't boil your
Water twice. Mark my words, Vladimir.
It's all about 'heavy water'! Bad for you. Heavy water is used for
Atomic weapons. The Doctor says so. The Doctor's our friend.
He helped Mikhail Arkadievich, he's
From the military. Yes, he's a military man."

Marfa left us alone for a minute.

"Vladimir. You are an architect, an urban man. My being here,
In the city, is something of a joke. I came before the War. Like yesterday.
From Maslovka (the railway station) I came to
Kursky! Eyes wide open! A country girl! Afraid
To go to Sadovaya Station Hall. I spied me a Beer hall!
Foolish girl! Standing there, beaming my village smile.
They stared at me – a man and a woman! And they asked:

'You like beer, girl?'

"No. But maybe I could wash glasses, sweep the floor?
Within the week
A noble gentleman squeezed my hand!"

"Your Prince!"

"The King! Mikhail Arkadievich. He
Loved me passionately. I was so gorgeous."

"You still are…"

"He loved the girls! Young and beautiful. Sorry I'm so
Open. I watched him like the scientist I am. Men, as they get older!
No need to tell you. You're an adult. We often went to the theatre.
THEATRE BEGINS WITH A HANGER!
Who said that?"

"Who knows?"

"Stanislavsky. His little
Aphorism. He said it about my husband!"

"What?"

"The Lobby of the theatre, that was the Beginning and End of
My husband's performances. A cloak room Casanova, the little room run
By young girls! Taking my jacket off.
He said he'd wait for me by the hangers. At the end, getting my
Coat, I'd go home. Usually alone."

"What about Arthur!"

"So unlike his father,
I worry! He's twenty. But no girls.
Maybe you can introduce him to some pretty young architect?"

"He's got lots of girls at the Dance Club!"

"They're his dance friends! It's like a sport,
This dancing. My life with Mikhail Arkadievich began with just such a sport.
Tango. The love-dance. Let me tell you."

TEN
ARTHUR'S FATHER

Arthur's father – a military scientist
Working for the USSR.
An intellectual always in loyal lockstep.
1946, July 5. America.
ATOMIC TEST,
A World wide-open Demonstration!
Initiated by
    Mr. J. Robert Oppenheimer![12]
A form of legalization brought about by the American Congress.
It looked like the Atomic Bomb might lead to an era of
International arms race cooperation –
So many countries.
        And the USSR.
All of them involved in the formalities.
After breakfast lectures, explanations, preparations –
Under a specially constructed roof.
To listen to
The Task Force commander.

VICE ADMIRAL WILLIAM H.P. BLANDY[13]:

> *"Gentlemen!*
> *How are you? Are you ready*
> *For the LAUNCH! The WORK.*
> *Our real ANGEL – About to fly!*

> *Our first Atomic Bomb, GILDA!*
> *That's what we call her."*

Applause, applause! Whistles!
The Call of the wild, America! Gilda!
Fly us to the moon!

BLANDY:

> *"Gentlemen, this is the last time I'll say this.*
> *No cameras! Listen?*
> *We'll have our own scientific footage that'll be*
> *Collected immediately into great coloured ALBUMS*
> *For you all! A special gift! A souvenir of your time*
> *Here in a time of troubled waters."*

Applause. Many International hands!
Seemingly interested. But bored. Yes, bored.
Waiting.
They knew all about mushrooms.
Fingering their Atomic notes. Blank
Pages provided:

MIKHAIL ARKADIEVICH:

> *"Gentlemen. As a Soviet scientist,*
> *I want you to know that*
> *We are here because the Atomic Apostle –*
> *Oppenheimer – has invited us here."*

("I have a hemorrhoid," the gentleman from Westminster said.)

"On the Bomb's body, the Bomb's head!

"Our Gilda."

A SONOROUS ALARM RINGS OUT.

SECOND! THIRD! MASK! PROTECTIVE GLASSES!
HEADPHONES! CHECK THE KEYBOARD! GREEN?
STILL RED? GREEN!

Launch in Progress!
Hearing nothing? German headphones!
    Then!
    A hurricane in the ears.
They closed their eyes. Seeing through flaming red lids,
A dry, parching red.
    Panic!
    Launch going on!
    THE HOME FIRES OF HELL
    (Dante. His Inferno! Too simple!).

> *"My husband had no interest in the theatre,*
> *The plays as such.*
> *He just wanted to dawdle*
> *Around with the girls,*
> *A little tawdry touching, fondling*
> *Between the hangers.*

I would sometimes catch him,
His hand cupping a breast.
He would wait for me to explode
In a rage. I never did. Which was
More frustrating for him than quick sex between the hangers."

ELEVEN
ATOMIC FRIENDSHIP

Test complete! All are free!
Delegates, representatives,
Spectators, official observers…

A catastrophe imprinted
In their nerves, eyes, ears…
Two Soviet delegates surveil each other while
Waiting for a ferry to a floating hotel where the Blast
Guests have their staterooms,
The Ocean Ship Hotel.

MIKHAIL ARKADIEVICH:

>*"My head is exploding. The Pacific.*
>*Swells and rolls.*
>*Pushkin's river Neva, from* The Bronze Horseman.
>*LIKE A SICK MAN IN HIS ROLLING BED."*

COMRADE VLASOV:

>*"Pushkin? Mikhail*
>*Arkadievich, we've got to get some sleep in this*
>*Our rocking cradle. A Soviet sleep of the just."*

They heard a woman's soothing voice:

BIKINI RADIO:

> *"Attention!*
> *The flame from the bomb has produced a fog!*
> *Blistered by colour.*
> *No radiation!*
> *HEAR!*
> *No radiation! Radiation! Radiation!*
> *ATTENTION! This is Bikini Radio!"*

COMRADE VLASOV:

> *"I've got no energy.*
> *I need to sleep."*

MIKHAIL ARKADIEVICH:

> *"I'm going to go for a walk on deck."*

The sky, dark.

Chilly.

SHIP HOTEL –
AN ARROW – DOWN!

Leaning against
The bar.
Only men.

Women? Girls? No girls.
Only glasses, bottles, snacks, and money.
This is not Siberia nor Kazakhstan.
Mikhail Arkadievich looks around –

CINEMA.
American air-conditioning.
Groping, he touched a seat,
Plush, and plunked himself down. Much more pleasant than the
Lecture seats, so Swedish-functional.
He decided he'd never want to be Swedish.
On screen, a dancing woman. Full
Buttocks, yet lithe.
The beer's so good. "White & Red Brew."
No hammer, no sickle. Slogan-free.

Mikhail Arkadievich's eyes are locked on the screen.
The Atomic Bomb.
GILDA –
MIKHAIL ARKADIEVICH whispering in his
New-found neighbour's ambassadorial ear:

> *"Please! What's the name of this movie? Gilda? Thanks.*
> *And the actress? Spell for me please!"*

> *"AR – EE – TEE – EH? – "*

Hotel Stateroom, # 112
A sofa – his bed. A television. He pushes the button.

Bikini TV. News. A Bikini girl describing the
1946 fashions. Mikhail Arkadievich smiling.

Flipping channels. Old black and white. Grainy.

"Gilda! We come to you! Bikini! Where are you?"

Mikhail Arkadievich. Closes his eyes. Sees
Everything is what it is as he drifts off into slumber sight. TANGO.
She dances in and out of the dark,

*"Such a woman. I've never seen such a woman in our Art
Theatre cloakrooms."*

Her face a slur of masks.
Dancing, a temptress, alluring.
Men around her! Not allowed to touch her gown!
But allowed to leer.
Mikhail Arkadievich feels his heart stop.

"What are you doing? Gilda!"

She looks at him! Yes!
She looks to him!
Does she hear his voice?
Does she remember seeing him before the Atomic Bomb blast?

HER VOICE:

"Mikhail Arkadievich!"

HE:

"Gilda?"

Then:

Knock knock! He hears a knock.

SHE:

"Don't open the door! That is Johnny! With his thugs!"

Knock! Heavier!
Mikhail Arkadievich opens his eyes.
The movie reels. Dancing Gilda.
Knock!
It is a really real knock. Gilda has fallen, she kneels.

GILDA to Johnny:

"Please, let me go! Leave me alone!"

Knock!

MIKHAIL ARKADIEVICH (half-dazed):

"Who's there?"

PHILIP:

*"It's me.
Philip! Your movie house neighbour?"*

MIKHAIL ARKADIEVICH:

"Wait. I'll turn off the movie. I was napping, dreaming."

PHILIP:

*"I've just had a Margarita Cocktail in the Bar.
It's a cocktail dedicated to her. Gilda. Rita Hayworth."*

MIKHAIL ARKADIEVICH:

*"Gilda, my lullaby. She put me to sleep.
I fell in love. And SHE – she took
ME away, entirely out of myself. Or maybe, into myself."*

Philip stands smiling.
Near a framed photo of a smiling baby.

PHILIP:

"Such a beautiful child, your youngest?"

MIKHAIL ARKADIEVICH:

"My only. My son. I married late."

PHILIP:

"His name?"

MIKHAIL ARKADIEVICH:

"Arthur. We Russians use your names, too."

PHILIP::

"Really? King Arthur?"

MIKHAIL ARKADIEVICH:

"My passion for your history might surprise you. A Soviet
Military physicist – your ancient Camelot.
King Arthur! Guinevere. And Lancelot.
Arthur's bravest knight."

PHILIP:

> *"Bravo! Let's get a balalaika! Fly into the Russian sky!*
> *Eisenstein's Ivan the Terrible. Marlene Dietrich as a German*
> *Playing a German, the*
> *Young Catherine. The start of her Hollywood career."*

MIKHAIL ARKADIEVICH:

> *"And we also have the 'Holy Grail.'*
> *The same legends, your Celts, Saxons. And our*
> *Northern Russians – the Vikings."*

PHILIP:

> *"Ah-h! A common ethnic culture? You are a diplomat!*
> *It's absolutely right that you should be here at this Round Table!"*

MIKHAIL ARKADIEVICH:

> *"No joke, Philip. After this Atomic Show we need to*
> *think how to bind ourselves together."*

PHILIP:

> *"Workers of the World Unite!"*

MIKHAIL ARKADIEVICH:

"After Gilda – *we'll find a way."*

PHILIP:

"But I think you need to go back to sleep, Mikhail."

MIKHAIL ARKADIEVICH:

"What can I say?"

TWELVE
GILDA

While shaving
I heard the phone ring in the common corridor.

> *"Morning, Vladimir.*
> *I am happy, you're still home.*
> *I am off to an early lecture.*
> *Tonight? Are you free?*
> *Remember we couldn't watch Gilda*
> *Without my mother.*
> *Well, she's off visiting the peasant*
> *Ladies of Maslovka."*

Arthur's curtained room. Semi-darkness.
Arthur's witchcraft moment,
His film projector, his Pandora's box,
Up and working.

ARTHUR:

> *"Will this be your first Hollywood experience?*

VLADIMIR:

> *"Maybe you're too young. In*
> *Kazakhstan, I saw a lot of films. The ones Hitler loved."*

ARTHUR:

"Oh, my God! Your life, it's the history of the USSR!"

VLADIMIR:

"I'll sing you a school song in German:

'Ich bin ein young pionier
Und unser fan ist red…'

ARTHUR:

"Hitler. America. Noir and more noir."

The screen on the wall.
Tango. Shades of
Black upon black. Silhouette figures
Stealing through the screen.

VLADIMIR:

"Where's Gilda?"

A man
Holds a gun to Johnny's head –
A thug – wanting Johnny's money.
A cane in the hands of a man who
Rescues Johnny –

ARTHUR:

> *"This is so foolish!"*

Casino tables.
Green has become
Grey on the screen. Tango tango,
A woman's vibrant voice. Johnny's face – Stop,
Action.
Whirling abstract lines! CRACK
   The screen as a dark hole.

VLADIMIR:

> *"What happened?"*

ARTHUR:

> *"The first fifteen minutes. Reloading. It's not*
> *Fellini. But my father liked this movie."*

VLADIMIR:

> *"Where's Gilda?"*

She hears her name.
She smiles. Lascivious on the edge of contempt.
Impenetrable eyes.
CLOSE-UP.

Long hair
Falling to her shoulders.
Shadows, concealed meaning
In and out of shades of black. Implied light.

ARTHUR:

"A small break?"

VLADIMIR:

"Are we short for time!"

ARTHUR:

"Tea. In two minutes."

A shining electric kettle on a
Kholmogory[14] tray, smell of the grass of Maslovka.
Sipping, we re-enter the screen.

Tango. Men with wine glasses.
Elegant. Clipped dialogue.
The interior dissolving.
A spiralling woman!

VLADIMIR:

"Gilda!"

Her body in flight.
Rotation.
World on its own axis.
Her come-hither
Smile. Her scorn, somehow implied.

BEHIND THE SCENES

ARTHUR:

> *"What happened? Behind the scenes? Why?*
>
> *"WHO IS THIS GILDA?*
> *RITA HAYWORTH?"*

VLADIMIR:

> *"What's going on?"*

ORSON WELLES, his voice:

> *"ONE OF THE SWEETEST WOMEN*
> *THAT EVER LIVED."*

Orson was once her lover.
Tormented Rita!
Also.
Early aggressive sex.

Beginning with
Her first dance partner – her father – Eduardo.

ARTHUR:

    "Stop!"

HER disappearance – launched into Heaven
On the head of the Atomic Bomb, dear Gilda.
At age of forty-two, Alzheimer's disease already taking hold,
    About to ravage her mind.
An autumnal life.

RONALD REAGAN, May 15, 1987:

    "RITA HAYWORTH WAS ONE OF OUR COUNTRY'S
    MOST BELOVED STARS.
    NANCY AND I ARE SADDENED BY RITA'S DEATH.
    SHE WAS A FRIEND WHO WE WILL MISS…"

VLADIMIR:

    "Look, she's dancing in the Casino!"

Argentina.
Stacks of poker chips.
Roulette wheels. Steel balls.
Numbers. Red. Black.
WWII.

Nazi criminals on the run.
New identities.
> Where is Gilda?
> GILDA!
> She is RITA!
Wartime Pinup!
Martyr, Magdalena.
The Margarita Cocktail.

Mexican Tequila. Salt on the rim.
Ice! More ice!
> A recipe
> Inspired by her time in Tijuana
> Where she'd danced as a teenager
> With her father.
> Now all of America drinks Margarita Cocktails!
> 1946 – SHE – as astonished Star –
> Belongs to all Americans,
> Including the military with their Atomic Weapon.
They painted HER on the walls of their barracks.
In the dark, they dreamed of HER on their hard mattresses,
Beneath thin cotton blankets.
There she was, wearing only her negligée.

RITA HAYWORTH:

> *"No one asked if they could put my body on the bomb!*
> *I am a citizen of these United States.*

Working seriously within American Culture!
Hey, America! Where are my First Amendment rights?
My breasts, my buttocks, speak volumes.
Where is the Constitution when I need it?

"Helpless! Stuck on my movie set!
I am Gilda! And you, Ms. Ellis,
My singing stand-in! I am a dancer — following a Scenario.
Why do I need you to sing?"

CHARLES VIDOR, director:

"Rita! Just keep repeating — 'I'm Gilda'!"

RITA HAYWORTH:

"I can't remember the words!
A lot of words. I am so unhappy around men.
I am alone. My only love was Orson!"

ORSON WELLES:

"You are my love — my very love!"

RITA HAYWORTH:

"He told me. 'I go to Bed with Gilda, but in the morning,
The light is all Rita Hayworth.'"

ORSON WELLES:

"She drove up into the hills, suicidal. She is beautiful.
She is who she is.
And who she is we'll never know."

RITA HAYWORTH:

"My only friend was Marlene Dietrich. During the War!"

MARLENE DIETRICH:

"Herald Tribune! November 17, 1942!

"ACTRESSES MARLENE DIETRICH AND
RITA HAYWORTH SERVING FOOD
TO SOLDIERS AT THE HOLLYWOOD CANTEEN..."

EXCLUSIVE Behind The Scenes.

RITA HAYWORTH:

"Thanks for our past together, you're so elegant,
So smart, my German Frau.
Your wild foxy face! Are you a real woman?
Or just a shade on the screen? I love the way sex for you
Was like Three-card Monte − find the pea −
With you wearing that male suit and tie −
So my confession − I can say this to you −

I GOT THE BEST HEAD EVER—
Not from a man – but from you – Marlene Dietrich.
And I returned The favour! And I told her – oh! – 'Mañana.'"

ORSON WELLES:

> "She'd fly into these rages, never at me, never once,
> Always at her father or her mother or her brother.
> She would break all the furniture and she'd get in a car
> And I'd have to get in the car and try to control her.
> She'd drive up into the hills, suicidally."

ARTHUR:

> "My Pandora's box!"

GILDA:

> "I came. I am near you."

JOHNNY:

> "I thought we had agreed that women and gambling didn't mix."

GILDA:

> "Remember me? Gilda, your wife. Remember?
> You haven't been around lately. Got a light?
> (She stoops to light her cigarette.)

"You don't look so hot, you know that?
You were never honest with me."

JOHNNY:

"Be realistic! You had such a full life up until now.
I gave you time to think."

GILDA:

"You're cockeyed, Johnny, all cockeyed. I figured that's
What the deal was."

Gilda's song!
Roar of the drunken men! Casino roulette!

Also, a suddenly different loud noise.
Arthur and Vladimir look at each other!

ARTHUR:

"Oh Christ! She's here!"

VLADIMIR:

"Who?"

GALINA IVANOVNA's Voice:

> *"Arthur! Arthur! Are you home?"*

ARTHUR:

> (He cannot shut down the sound quickly enough!)
> *"Yes! We're home!"*

Galina Ivanovna opens the door to Arthur's room.

SHE:

> *"And Vladimir's here!*
> (She tries to smile)
> *"Hello hello, Vladimir!*
> (She steps into the room)
> *"Oh, my son! You're watching* Gilda?
> *And you've turned the sound off? But she is dancing anyway!"*

ARTHUR:

> *"Mama! Relax!"*

SHE:

> *"My son! You're so difficult."*

ARTHUR:

"Mama."

SHE:

"You're at the end, the lovely scene with the gloves!
Switch on the sound!
We loved this moment! Your father and I."

ARTHUR:

"If you want, we can go back to the beginning."

SHE:

"Shut up! I need to sit. Is this water?
Not wine? My heart! Thank you. Vladimir."

VLADIMIR:

"Better, Galina Ivanovna?"

SHE:

"Not so good. But better. My question to you,
As an adult and as an intelligent young man,
Why is there this theatrical étude in the movie –
This slow taking off of the gloves?

Back then, it was called pornographic –
In the Capitalist International press!"

ARTHUR:

"And in our USSR!"

SHE:

"Shut up. You know we are different.
I'm talking to Vladimir!"

(Rita Hayworth dancing, singing – dubbed by Ms. Ellis:

"Put the blame on Mame
Mame kissed a buyer from out of town
That kiss burned Chicago down…")

GALINA IVANOVNA:

"Oh, my God! Amazing! I hear Stanislavsky's I BELIEVE!
His adoration in that song. Tea, yes. With black chokeberry jam."

THIRTEEN
A SCOLIOSIS MOMENT

Vladimir's home
By Paveletsky Station. No noise
From the trains –
He's got a good rest.
Stretching out on a new hard mattress that
Helps his scoliosis.
After his Pandora escapade, some shut-eye.
Swooping dreams.
Arthur's father in the cloakroom
At the Moscow Theatre.
Vladimir is wary, a little afraid of Gilda.
Tango on a cloud!
Rita has stolen his brain. How else to explain?

PANDORA:

"Hello!"

VLADIMIR:

"I, Vladimir, am asleep."

PANDORA:

*"Pretend this is your dream.
In reality, you are inside my box."*

"Are you alone? On your hard mattress?"

Teasing Vladimir, trying to rouse him,
Gilda, peels her second glove! Tango!
Bare –
Striptease!

MIKHAIL ARKADIEVICH:

"Can you see me, Gilda?
I'm in your movie? Touch my hand!"

Gilda turns to Mikhail Arkadievich, tears in her eyes!

MR. VIDOR:

"That is one of the best shooting sessions ever."

Put the blame on Mame
Mame kissed a buyer from out of town
That kiss burned Chicago down…

Mikhail Arkadievich is shocked.
How could this have happened?
This accusatory footage.
He's had no time to get ready.
The *Gilda* movie is in his luggage.
And the photo album.
His son will be TWO tomorrow!

MIKHAIL ARKADIEVICH:

"I am not just a Soviet physicist
But am now an American movie actor! It's hard work,
Like Siberia, like Kazakhstan.
Being a movie star is
A kind of exile...
Chapeau!"

VLADIMIR:

"I am awake in my sleep:
Someone is asking
If I've heard from the Cat?"

FOURTEEN
AIRPLANE SCENE

SHE:

"Started out as a dance partner for her father, age twelve.
Being submissive, she gave him all her talent. And more.
As a dancer, she became known as Casino Margarita.
Gravitated to many men who controlled and used her
In one sleaze way or another.
On the silver screen, she found fame!
A Wartime Hollywood Star.
Her Life Magazine negligée photo pinned up
On millions of bedroom walls."

EXCLUSIVE Behind The Scene:

Yes, a real aeroplane!
A Soviet aircraft – "IL-18" Flight over the ocean.
Two rows of seats. Comfortable?
Much better than "TU 104."
And the service is better. Not just tea. Also coffee,
And caviar sandwiches. Wine? Crimean. No International vintages.
Vodka? Stolichnaya.
Special air hostesses –
Slavic butterflies.
Nobody laughs.

You see the sunlit land through the clouds.
Moscow under silver wings!
There is in fact a giant Cat standing at the end of
Vnukovo landing strip!

Gilda is here – aka Rita Hayworth –
Chekhov's *Three Sisters* on her lap. Lips moving,
Repeating repeating repeating
Someone's father is dancing down the aisle, singing:

> *"Dance dance, Margarita!*
> *In Argentina! In New York!*
> *Over Moscow, the cranes are flying!*
> *In her own nest, a pregnant stork."*

"If I die I will be part of life in one way or another…

The plane sets down! Dizziness, nausea!

"If I die I will be part of life in one way or another…

"If I die I will be part of life in one way or another…"

The man dancing down the aisle of the plane!
He's not Gilda's father, not Eduardo –

He is, yes, yes Mikhail Arkadievich – well-known Soviet physicist.

Coming back on this flight from Bikini Atoll,
You came back with him:

"If I die I will be part of life in one way or another…

"If I die I will be part of life in one way or another…"

Soviet passengers applauding!

MIKHAIL ARKADIEVICH:

> *"Gilda Gilda! Who knows where SHE is?"*

> *"The Customs Officers of the USSR!"*

> *"Where are you?"*

Mikhail Arkadievich hears his name called!

A huge bouquet hides GALINA IVANOVNA's face:

> *"O, my loving Mikhail Arkadievich!"*

MIKHAIL ARKADIEVICH:

> *"Oh, my God! Am I back?"*

GALINA IVANOVNA:

"I am so happy! You came in time, my dear!
Arthur's Birthday! Calling for 'papa'!"

MIKHAIL ARKADIEVICH:

"O, my God!"

GALINA IVANOVNA:

"Yes! You are in Moscow. I got us tickets for
Uncle Vanya! At your beloved Art Theatre!"

MIKHAIL ARKADIEVICH:

"Where is SHE?
GILDA! We were to work together
Down among the hangers in Wardrobe."

GALINA IVANOVNA:

"What're you talking about? Mikhail Arkadievich?"

MIKHAIL ARKADIEVICH:

"Gilda!"

EDUARDO CANSINO:

"Dance dance Margarita!
In Argentina! In New York!
The cranes are flying!
In Moscow, a nesting pregnant stork."

FIFTEEN
A HOMECOMING OF SORTS

Nighttime in the city. No traffic
Sadovaya Ring, Main Line.
The Department of Atomic Energy's chauffeur-driven car,
Moving at a full speed. No limit on Moscow roads.
Open windows – a couple in the back seat
Breathing the chilly Soviet air.
1946: Moscow streets at night are empty.
Rita is under police surveillance,
The chauffeur smiles knowingly.

He can see in the rear-view mirror
What looks like
Behemoth the Cat,
Mikhail Arkadievich bids *"Good evening"* to
Gilda and Rita as they set off
Side-saddle, into the noosphere,
Each on her own
Slender missile, the war-head
Throbbing in the air.
Westbound for Hollywood, the entertainment atoll.

Mikhail Arkadievich opens his eyes and
Cries out to the concierge,

"Good evening. The evening is good.
Time for a cocktail at home, a Rita-Margarita,
Skip the plain old vodka with a pickle."

The elevator works. All the way to the fourth floor.
In the doorway,
Smiling Marfa is shushing: *"Shh, shh, shh!*

"Yes – Arthur's asleep! Poor little boy,"

Galina Ivanovna takes off her shoes and tiptoes into their future.
Mikhail Arkadievich says:

"Shh…something's afoot."   MEOW

MARFA, who never says anything, is suddenly singing, very quietly:

"Sleep, sleep beauty bright,
Dreaming in the night,
Sleep, sleep, in sleep
Little sorrows sit and weep."

Mikhail Arkadievich is snoring –
The telephone is on the carpet beside his shoes
Their white caoutchouc[15] soles.
Mama is in her kitchen wearing a
Brightly coloured silk dressing gown. She's happy.
A dutiful Soviet scientist:

"Do you KNOW that a LAW
Concerning Conservation Energy was discovered by our
Mikhail Vasilyevich Lomonosov?[16] *Not by that Frenchman Lavoisier!*
He came late, seventeen years later!
Conservation by contraction, the contraction of time."

On the Line,

RITA calls her friend Marlene:

"All I wanted was just what everybody else wants,
You know, to be loved."

And FRAULEIN replies:

"Darling, my legs aren't so beautiful,
I just know what to do with them."

I Remember Chekhov's aphorism:

"Brevity is a sister to talent."

Rita. Margarita. Rio-Rita.
Anton Chekhov's *Uncle Vanya*
Playbook in hand,
And SONYA cries:

"What can we do? We must live out our lives."

In this period of
The progressive mechanics of dialectical materialism
Gone to seed, what's to be done?
We end up doing what we do.
Arthur is in America!
American Computer at the University of Pennsylvania.
Arthur's mama flew to Germany for the
Privatization of a Sugar Plant.
Mikhail Arkadievich decided to meet up with
GildaRita on the Sunset Strip.

Bikini Atoll is now known
For the BIKINI designed
By the French-American
Automobile Engineer, LOUIS RÉARD,
Made popular by that leading existentialist,
Brigitte Bardot last seen
Astride Picasso's goat.

This has come to pass. Also,
We are celebrating with an
ATOMIC CAKE baked by Arthur's ancient Aunty – Marfa!

Rita removes her long glove.
She undresses her hand,
Finger by finger,
A scene censured as too suggestive
In several countries.

"A drink, a drink to my stripling youth,
I remember thawing out during the Thaw.
I was, by all accounts, country uncouth.
I'd come up from Kazakhstan,
Learning to act with aplomb
Over cocktails, cake, and the Atomic Bomb."

Cocktail Preparation:
140ml of Tequila.
60ml of Cointreau.
30ml of lime juice.
Ice.
Salt the edges of the glass.
And a straw!

"And beside my glass – Magic! A slice of
ATOMIC CAKE –

"Do you have a recipe?"

"It's on Google."

"We are all on Google."

"So we should be. It's where we deserve to be."

Set a layer of banana cake on a cake plate.
Top with a slice of banana, then spread banana pudding over the top.
Spread whipped cream over pudding. Place a layer of chocolate cake on top.

Sprinkle with grated chocolate. Cover with strawberries.
Then spread with whipped cream. Place a layer of white cake on top.
Frost the top of the cake with generous dollops of whipped cream.
Refrigerate.

Wait fifteen minutes.

Which is
No time at all.
In a world of

Indiscriminate period fire.

.

    . .

.   .

          .

    .

    .   .

END NOTES

[1] Main political and theatrical show hall in the Kremlin.

[2] Illegal publishers of banned literature in the USSR, 1960-1980. The name comes from Russian words that mean, roughly speaking, "self-publishing."

[3] The Russian theatre focussed on the Stanislavsky's System. Founded by K. Stanislavsky and V. Nemirouvch-Danchenko in 1898.

[4] A major character in the novel, *The Master and Margarita*, by Mikhail Bulgakov (1891-1940).

[6] A Russian monthly literary magazine. In the Sixties, it took up a dissident position.

[7] Soviet movie, *Battleship Potemkin* (1925), by S. Eisenstein; it had enormous world-wide influence on modernism, not just on filmmakers but on poets, painters, and novelists.

[8] Isaac Babel, important soviet writer, literary translator, historian and Bolshevik revolutionary, July 1894-January 1940.

[9] Petrovka is a downtown Moscow street.

[10] A Moscow railway station.

[11] Leonid Brezhnev, First Secretary of the Communist Party of the Soviet Union, 1964-1982, years that came to be known as the period of "Brezhnev Stagnation."

[12] J. Robert Oppenheimer, American theoretical physicist; director of the Los Alamos Laboratory during the Manhattan Project; responsible for the research and design of an atomic bomb; known as the "father of the atomic bomb."

[13] H.P. Blandy was known for overseeing the atomic bomb tests at Bikini Island in the Pacific Ocean. He once said, "I am not an atomic playboy, exploding these bombs to satisfy my personal whims."

[14] Kholmogory handicrafts practiced in the villages of Kholmorsky District, Arkhangelsk Oblast.

[15] Unvulcanized natural rubber.

[16] Mikhail Vasilyevich Lomonosov (1711–1765), Russian physicist.

ACKNOWLEDGEMENTS

I thank Bruce Meyer for his editorial direction with *On "The Death of Ivan Ilyich"* and Barry Callaghan for his translations and his attention to detailing throughout the three books.

BOOKS BY VLADIMIR AZAROV

Winter in the Country
On "The Death of Ivan Ilyich"
An Atomic Cake
  Three Books (2019, Exile Editions)

Of Architecture: The Territories of a Mind (2016, Exile Editions)
  • with illustrations by Nina Bunjevac

Sochi Delirium (2014, Exile Editions)

Broken Pastries (2014, Exile Editions)

Seven Lives (2014, Exile Editions)

Strong Words: Poetry in a Russian and English Edition (2013, Exile Editions)
  • co-translated with Barry Callaghan

Mongolian Études (2013, Exile Editions)

Night Out (2013, Exile Editions)

Dinner with Catherine the Great (2012, Exile Editions)

***

Voices in Dialogue (2011, BookThug)

The Kiss from Mary Pickford (2011, BookThug)

Imitation (2011, BookThug)

Of Life & Other Small Sacrifices (2010, BookThug)

***

26 Letters, Poems, Pictures (2009, Probel-2000)

Black Square (2009, Probel-2000)

My Bestiary (2009, Probel-2000)

Graphics of Life (2009, Probel-2000)

IMAGES

Winter in the Country : A drawing by Alexandre Pushkin, from his notebooks.

On "The Death of Ivan Ilyich" : *Man directs time spiral with hand,* illustration by Bruce Rolff.

An Atomic Cake : Admiral William H.P. Blandy and his wife cut into a mushroom cloud cake, celebrating the 1946 atomic tests on Bikini Atoll.